# SECRET
# MOTIVES

ALSO BY ERICK LEITHE

*What Lies Can Do*

# SECRET MOTIVES

**ERICK LEITHE**

bookhouse
PUBLISHING

bookhouse
PUBLISHING

2950 Newmarket St., Suite 101-358 | Bellingham, WA 98226
Ph: 206.226.3588 | www.bookhouserules.com

*Secret Motives*
Copyright © 2022 by Erick Leithe

The information provided in this book is for entertainment purposes only. It is
not intended to be a source of financial advice. Creating a financial strategy or
plan or making adjustments to one should be undertaken only after consulting
with a professional. The publisher and the author make no guarantee of
financial results obtained by using information in this book.

10 9 8 7 6 5 4 3 2 1

Printed in the United States of America

Library of Congress Control Number: 2022916106

ISBN: 978-1-952483-57-8 (Paperback)
ISBN: 978-1-952483-58-5 (eBook)

*Editors: Christine Breen & Julie Scandora*
*Cover design: Scott Book*
*Book design: Melissa Vail Coffman*

*To my family,*
*with love*

For who makes you different from anyone else?
What do you have that you did not receive?
And if you did receive it,
why do you boast as though you did not?

– 1 Corinthians 4:7

# PROLOGUE

JOHN AND SUSAN STALEY had no idea what was about to happen to them. On a mid-September morning, they had driven nineteen miles south from their Paramus, New Jersey, home to Newark to catch the train to Boston. They planned to celebrate their wedding anniversary over a long weekend on Cape Cod. John's brother and wife would pick them up at the train station, and the four of them would drive to an inn at the seaside town of Chatham.

The Staleys sat in the large waiting room at Newark's Penn Station, waiting for the 9:33 a.m. Amtrak express that would deliver them to Boston's South Station by 1:45 p.m. They were reading books that each had brought for the four-hour train ride. People filled the parallel wooden benches, waiting to travel north to New York City and Boston or south to Philadelphia and Washington, DC. John put his arm around his wife and kissed her on the cheek. They looked forward to spending several days at the ocean.

A man came running toward them, carrying a large, slender package. Dressed in a business suit, he appeared to be in his fifties.

He stopped in front of them, panting. Leaning over, gasping for breath, he said, "I'm in danger. Please hold onto this package."

"What?!" John exclaimed.

"Keep this for me," he replied, handing the package to John.

"What's this all about?" John asked.

"Do you live in Newark?" he asked.

"No."

"Where then?" The man was clearly in distress.

"Paramus," John replied.

"I need help," he said. "They're trying to steal this. People are chasing me."

"What is it?"

"It's important. Please. Please help me," the man said. "Write your e-mail address on my ticket, and I'll get in touch with you. I have to leave." He held out his ticket to John.

"What's your name?" Susan asked, somewhat upset.

"That's not important now. Please give me your e-mail address."

The man looked as if he were a solid citizen in a desperate situation. Reluctantly, John took the ticket, wrote his e-mail address on it, and handed it back to the distressed stranger. The man turned and raced toward the platform.

The Staleys looked at each other.

"What a start to our holiday," John said.

"You can say that again!" Susan responded. "What do we do with the package?"

"I guess we take it with us."

———◆———

DURING THEIR HOLIDAY at Chatham on the Cape, the Staleys kept the package in their suitcase and left it under the bed. Susan periodically checked on it throughout the day. A couple of days later, they returned to Paramus with the package safe inside their suitcase.

After their weekend holiday, the Staleys placed the unopened package on a corner shelf in their basement, expecting to be contacted by the man in the suit. However, they never heard from him again. After a while, they forgot about it, and the package lay covered by a slight film of dust.

After fourteen years, John Staley died. Susan passed away six years later. Their only child, Reverend James Staley, became the executor of their modest estate. The unopened box was found by Jim when he flew from California to plan his mother's memorial service and tend to his parents' belongings in their one-story house. He stayed in Paramus for a week after the service to complete his list of things to do. His first task involved taking careful inventory of his parents' possessions on the main floor, accumulated during their fifty-six years of marriage. Among them, he identified family records and meaningful keepsakes that he would ship back to the Bay Area. He had scheduled an estate sale with a local company for the rest of the items: furniture, books, and clothing. He also planned to call Goodwill and ask them to take what they wanted from the basement. What was left would go into the dumpster he had rented to collect debris from a few remodeling projects he had scheduled with a local contractor. He hoped to list the house for sale in two months.

Sorting the items in the basement was the last activity on his list. He dreaded the job of going through the shelves of additional belongings stored by his parents and deciding what items to keep and what to discard.

There was a reason young Jim Staley had spent little time in his parents' unfinished basement. Its fate had been determined when he was the age of five. He was alone there because his mother had been called upstairs by a telephone call. A cat had peered through an open window, hissed at him, and then jumped onto a table below. The unexpected intrusion both surprised and frightened him, causing him to dash up the stairs. It took a while for his mother to catch the cat and remove it from the house. Thereafter, he avoided going to the basement. He much preferred playing with his toys on the large rug in the upstairs living room, where his mother would bring him occasional snacks. As a teenager, he even kept his Boy Scout gear and sports equipment in the garage so he wouldn't have to go down to the basement.

Now with a combination of uneasiness and sadness, Staley finally descended the stairs to review the leftovers from his parents' long marriage. One wall had two long shelves. On the top shelf, his mother had kept an assortment of stored goods: a suitcase full of her discarded apparel that she didn't want to give away, several boxes of Christmas decorations, jars of strawberry and raspberry jam, canned vegetables, and a collection of empty boxes of various sizes. She wanted just the right box if she had a particular item she needed to mail to someone. On one end of the lower shelf, his father had kept a supply of cans of motor oil, along with various tools he had inherited, such as saws, crowbars, and hammers that he never used.

As a teenager, Staley had tried to imagine how the basement would appear if it were finished, with paneled walls, ceiling tiles, and a wood floor covering the concrete. There could even be a guest bedroom. With a sofa or two and some easy chairs, along with a TV, it had the potential to be a party area for three or four couples from his school on Saturday nights, but he never suggested these ideas to his parents because he knew they couldn't afford to remodel the basement.

Standing in front of the shelving, he hoped to find a childhood memento among the articles in the basement that he could take back with him to California. As he opened the boxes of decorations, he recalled memories of past Christmases with his parents. He selected a couple of tree ornaments and a stuffed Santa Claus, one-foot tall, that he placed in a paper sack. The canned food could go to a local food bank. Maybe the next-door neighbor would like the cans of motor oil. He would ask the company managing the estate sale to include his mother's apparel in the suitcase with her clothing from the upstairs bedroom. One of the last items he examined was a thin box, about two feet by two feet, at the far end of the lower shelf.

He carried the package to a nearby table beneath a window where he could see it in a better light. Cutting the twine that secured the box, he carefully lifted off the top. Beneath some newspapers, he saw something that made him catch his breath. It appeared to be an ancient scroll of some sort. The scroll looked very old and fragile, and the writing appeared to be in Hebrew script. Why was it there in the basement? How had his parents acquired it? Why hadn't they mentioned it? These were questions he pondered as he stared at the object in front of him.

The last thing he expected to find in his parents' dusty basement was a box containing an ancient artifact.

# 1

IT WAS JUST ANOTHER MORNING, until he unfolded the newspaper. Sitting at the kitchen table, Matt Beringer froze in his chair when he saw the headline on the front page of the *East Bay Times*. His heart raced as he read the article. After several minutes, he put the paper down and sat back in his chair. "Jancy, you won't believe what's in today's paper! An article about Pastor Staley!"

"You mean Jim Staley, your boss?" she asked.

"Yes! Listen to this," he said, picking up the paper again. "The headline says, 'East Bay Minister Inherits Priceless Dead Sea Scroll.'" He stared at the paper, shaking his head. "This is incredible!"

Jancy reached for the paper. "That sounds rather strange. Pastor Staley connected to a Dead Sea Scroll?" She read, while Matt sat opposite her, trying to absorb the surprising news.

"What's even more shocking is that the article says it's the Esther Scroll! Esther being the only Old Testament book that was never found among the scrolls discovered in the Qumran caves in the 1940s and 1950s. Finding this missing book is unbelievable!"

"The only Esther Scroll that's ever been found? Seriously?"

"Yes. If it's authentic," Matt said, "it would be the first one. If it's genuine, it could be worth a fortune!"

"How did he inherit it?" she asked. "From his parents?"

"Yes, from his parents! His mother died a few months ago, and he went back to New Jersey for the memorial service. He never mentioned anything about inheriting a scroll," Matt said. "I'm stunned!"

"I can't believe he'd want this kind of publicity," Jancy said.

"I agree," Matt said. "The article has a surreal quality to it. Do they have the right guy? Why would his parents own a Dead Sea Scroll?"

"The reporter has surely verified the story," she said, while her finger moved along each line of the article. "By the way, you made a great omelet this morning."

"Thanks. Just added some scallions to the usual ingredients." He stood and carried their empty plates to the sink. "You know, Jancy, I'm just blown away by this. I can't wait to hear what Pastor Staley has to say about the scroll at our staff meeting this morning."

"I'll tell you one thing for certain," she said, smiling. "I'll bet he never intended for it to become public."

"That's for sure. The article says his father was an educator and school principal for thirty-five years in Paramus, New Jersey. He died six years ago of Alzheimer's. His mother was a homemaker, and they had one son. Pastor Staley found the Esther Scroll in a box in his parents' basement. Unbelievable."

"They kept a Dead Sea Scroll in their basement?!"

"Exactly."

"The real story is *how* did the Staleys acquire a Dead Sea Scroll," Jancy said.

"The article doesn't say. It just doesn't fit," Matt said, "that Jim Staley's parents would own an ancient object like that."

"Do you know anything else about the scroll?"

"Not much more than what's covered in the article. It's a large fragment of the book of Esther, which makes it one-of-a-kind and very valuable."

"Why is it the first to be discovered?"

Matt took a sip from his glass of cranberry juice and leaned back in his chair. "I've known that the Esther Scroll was the only missing Old Testament book, and I've wondered why. I've heard a wide range of explanations," he said. "The easy answer is that Esther Scrolls existed, but they weren't stored with the others."

"Staley's scroll confirms that at least one was preserved."

"Yes, but the more interesting explanation has to do with the Qumran community, a monastic group of men from a deeply religious sect called the Essenes. The scrolls belonged to the Essenes, and they may have frowned on or rejected a book that doesn't refer to God."

"It doesn't refer to God?" Jancy asked.

"No. The book of Esther doesn't mention God's name."

"That's a little unusual, isn't it?"

"Yes. All the Old Testament books, except Esther and Song of Songs, refer to God's name. The other Old Testament books involve prophets who mention God or miracles where God is given credit, but not these two books. Compared with most Old Testament books, Esther is somewhat of an outlier."

"That's interesting. I think I want to read the book of Esther," she said, standing to finish clearing the table.

"It has a unique writing style. The author chose to show God at work in the narrative, protecting the Jews from being destroyed, but operating as an invisible hand. God is at work behind the curtains, so to speak."

"Never mentioned, but always in control," Jancy said.

"Right. Esther describes how God is always present with his people. The fact that the hero of the book is a young girl may be another reason why the book didn't appeal to the Essenes at Qumran, an all-male community. Another reason might have been their displeasure over Esther's marriage to a Persian king. Also, the setting might have been objectionable since most of the Old Testament is about Jewish history and customs. Esther's story occurred in the opulent courts of a foreign land and must have seemed strange to them."

"Why do people believe that Staley's scroll came from the Qumran area?"

"Several Hebrew scholars have authenticated it."

"Jim and Joan might need to worry about their personal safety, now that the public knows about it. It must have been leaked," she said.

"I agree. This news will complicate their lives."

"Matt, you're amazing. What don't you know?!" Jancy walked over and kissed him on the cheek.

"I know a fair amount about the Dead Sea Scrolls, although I'm a little fuzzy on the details," Matt said. "I've collected articles on them. If you have a few minutes before you leave for work, I'll grab my file and tell you more about the Essenes."

"Absolutely. I'd like to hear more!"

After a short time, Matt returned with a manila folder. "I read an article on the scrolls when I was in high school, and it really grabbed me. Along the way, I've collected a few more articles. Many scholars believe the Dead Sea Scrolls are the most important archaeological discovery of the twentieth century."

"What a find for Jim Staley!" she said.

"Very true. The Qumran community existed during Jesus's time," Matt said, looking at an article. "It was originally settled in the eighth century BCE and then abandoned after the Babylonian invasion and destruction of the First Temple in 586 BCE. Some scholars believe it was resettled around 150 BCE by some Essenes who were disaffected priests and members of the Jerusalem Temple. They didn't like the way the temple was being run."

"Does that mean the scrolls date from around the time of Jesus or earlier?"

"Yes," Matt said. "Scholars believe some of the scrolls came from the Jerusalem Temple, and a few of them might have been written at Qumran, so they're the oldest biblical documents in existence."

"It sounds like the Esther Scroll is a pretty important discovery," Jancy said. "How very odd that it was found in a basement in Paramus, New Jersey. A cave of its own!"

"Ha. Very clever, Jancy! It's estimated that the book of Esther might have been written in the fifth century BCE, but Staley's scroll could have been produced at Qumran during Jesus's time."

"It's like finding a missing piece to a jigsaw puzzle."

"Correct," Matt added. "I bet we're going to be hearing a lot more about the Dead Sea Scrolls in the months ahead."

"I wonder if they'll want to sell it," she said.

"So do I. It will be interesting to hear what they have in mind," Matt said, "and I'm sure he can't be happy about the newspaper article."

"Okay, love," Jancy said. "I need to go to work. I'm attending a workshop at First Pres in Berkeley for most of the day. I look forward to hearing what Jim Staley says about the scroll over dinner tonight."

"Great! I'm leaving for Hacienda in about fifteen minutes. See you after work."

It was the first Tuesday in August. After giving Matt a hug and a kiss, Jancy left their San Leandro apartment at eight o'clock for her job as director of children's ministries at the Montclair Presbyterian Church in Oakland, carrying a carrot cake she had purchased to celebrate the church secretary's birthday.

Matt remained at the kitchen table and finished reading the sports section of the newspaper. Collecting some papers from his desk in the living room, he headed to Hacienda Presbyterian Church in nearby San Lucas, taking a file with a draft of a sermon he was preparing for a worship service in early October. Matt had taken some ribbing from a few of his classmates at his graduation in May from San Francisco's Calvin Theological Seminary for accepting a full-time position at the wealthy East Bay church where he had interned the year before. San Lucas, with a population of around fifty thousand, was ranked seventy-third on *Fortune* magazine's list of America's Richest Towns. However, after their wedding in June, the newlyweds were adjusting to their life together in a modest one-bedroom apartment that Matt had rented in San Leandro.

Matt preferred to take a slower route to work, driving through residential neighborhoods with less traffic, rather than traveling on the Nimitz Freeway. Hacienda Presbyterian was just minutes away when he cruised through the San Lucas village and proceeded up Buena Vista Drive to the church on top of the hill. He arrived at around nine o'clock and found his usual parking space in the far corner of the large lot overlooking San Francisco Bay. The weekly staff meeting would convene at nine thirty.

The Hacienda church campus consisted of ten acres, donated by a wealthy member over seventy years ago, overlooking the town of San Lucas and San Francisco Bay. The congregation had built a mission-style sanctuary and adjacent bell tower, as well as a separate two-story administration building in the shape of a quadrangle, open at the end facing the bay. It housed the church office, ministers' offices, meeting rooms, and classrooms. A tile fountain sat at the open end of the quadrangle, near the main entrance to the building. The sanctuary was located to the north, a short distance away on a broad sidewalk that led to the church's entrance. The stained-glass windows on the west and east sides of the building that pointed north looked dark from the outside, but from the inside, they exploded with bright colors that radiated throughout the interior. The windows, originally used in French churches to communicate scenes and episodes from the Bible to everyone, even those uneducated, symbolize the Christian experience: a person must become engaged in the faith, rather than stand outside, to receive its blessings. The landscaped campus surrounding the sanctuary and administration building included a grass lawn, as well as mature trees and shrubs. The flat church parking lot was located to the west of the buildings, a few steps below the level campus.

On his way to his second-floor office in the administration quadrangle, Matt stopped at the church office to check his mailbox. He waved at Pastor Staley's administrative assistant, Evelyn Kirby, sitting at her desk behind the tall glass window of her corner office. His mailbox held a couple of envelopes and a magazine. Then he walked down the hall and ascended the stairs to his office that overlooked the courtyard. He also had a western view of San Francisco Bay. When he arrived each morning, he liked to open the leaded-glass window facing west and push aside the curtains, admitting a soft breeze. Bright sunlight streamed through the opening, bathing his office in a warm glow. He sat down at his desk and reviewed his calendar, which included meetings and appointments, along with a list of what he wanted to accomplish that day.

As a full-time staff member, Matt would be continuing his work with the middle school youth under the new position title of assistant minister. His job description had been expanded to include some involvement with the children's and high school ministries, but the specifics hadn't yet been described to him by his supervisor, Pastor Charles Boyle. Matt had learned during his internship, which had begun the previous September and ended in May, that Boyle didn't place a high priority on details. At a few minutes before nine thirty, Matt descended the stairs to attend the staff meeting in Pastor Staley's office at the end of the first-floor hallway.

Mrs. Kirby was sitting directly in front of the senior pastor's desk, so he took the chair to her right. Shortly thereafter, Pastor Boyle joined them, pulling up another chair to sit on her left. They waited for the arrival of Pastor Staley and Lisa Jacobson, director of children's ministries.

"Did you see the article about Pastor Staley in the morning paper?" Mrs. Kirby asked, turning to Matt with a half-smile, half-frown.

"Yes, I sure did," Matt said. "I was totally surprised! It's awesome! While I'm happy for him, I can't believe he wanted the public to know about it."

"I completely agree with you. Most unfortunate, if you ask me," she replied. "He's become an overnight celebrity! I'm sure that's not what he wanted."

"Jim just inherited an extremely valuable asset," Boyle interjected. "He now has the potential for a very comfortable retirement ahead of him when he sells the scroll. He'll probably announce his retirement to us in a few minutes."

Matt wasn't sure if Boyle was thinking about the senior pastor's good fortune or wishing instead that he had received the inheritance.

"I heard you, Charles," Staley said, entering his office with a slight smile on his face. "No retirement announcement today." He carried a cup of coffee as he crossed the room. Taking his seat behind the desk, he looked at each member of his staff. "Lisa won't be joining us today. She has an all-day workshop with other directors of children's ministries at First Presbyterian in Berkeley. Matt, I expect she'll see Jancy there."

"Jim, off the bat, can we say we all saw the article in the morning paper? That's some announcement!" Boyle said. "Did you know you were going to inherit a Dead Sea Scroll?" Boyle's interest in money and finance was never far below the surface.

Staley pushed his chair back from the desk and crossed his legs. "When I found the scroll in a box in my parents' basement, I was shocked. I knew it was a very old document but didn't know exactly what it was, so I contacted an Old Testament professor on the faculty at the Princeton Theological Seminary. I took it to Princeton to show him and a few of his colleagues. They verified that it was a large fragment of the book of Esther. They also referred me to some Jewish scholars in New York City who authenticated it."

"Did you give an interview to the *East Bay Times*?" Boyle asked, leaving no stone unturned.

"I certainly did not," Staley said, "and I'm not happy about the article. Someone shared the information with the newspaper without my approval, and I'd like to know who did it. It must have been provided by someone in my attorney's law firm or by the bank that's holding the scroll in safekeeping. I plan to speak with the *East Bay Times* and investigate who might have done it."

"What will you do with the scroll?" Boyle asked.

"We're not sure, Charles," Staley said. "I need to do some research on the subject. I expect we'll eventually sell it."

"Have you had the scroll appraised?" Boyle asked.

"I'm working on that," Staley responded.

"The phone has already started to ring with questions about the article," Mrs. Kirby said. "We'll need to be prepared for a barrage of phone calls and correspondence, at least for a while."

"You're probably right," Staley replied. "I never wanted to be famous, but the article will generate major publicity."

The three Hacienda staff members sat in silence, facing Staley, each contemplating the significance of the discovery of an ancient artifact two thousand years old.

"I was very happy with the way things were," Staley said, shaking his head. "I wasn't looking for more excitement in my life."

The rest of the staff meeting proceeded as usual. Staley reviewed the order of the worship service for the following Sunday at 9:30 a.m. and what roles Pastors Boyle and Beringer would play. He also discussed the staff picnic that was held every summer on the last Saturday in August at the Staleys' home. He confirmed that those present, in addition to Lisa Jacobson and her husband, planned to attend the picnic. Staley then asked Mrs. Kirby, Boyle, and Matt to share any travel plans they had for the remainder of the summer. Finally, Staley profiled a family that had recently moved to San Lucas and would be joining the church on Sunday, which would include the baptism of their youngest of three children. As the meeting concluded, he asked Matt if he would stay for a few minutes.

After Mrs. Kirby and Pastor Boyle left the room, Matt remained seated.

Staley took off his glasses and placed them on his desk. "For whatever reason, I've never spent much time reading about the Dead Sea Scrolls," Staley said, "but I plan to become an expert on them in the next year or so. I have no idea what to do with the scroll. I suppose I'll receive inquiries from people and institutions that are interested in buying it. I've been told that this fragment of the Esther Scroll may be worth well over a million dollars."

"My parents attended a Dead Sea Scrolls exhibit in Seattle a number of years ago," Matt said. "They also went to some associated lectures, and they were fascinated by what they heard. When I was in high school, their comments about the scrolls caused me to read an article about the Qumran community. I read a book about the scrolls during seminary, and I've collected some articles about them, so I have a little knowledge about the subject, if I can help."

"Yes, you might very well be of some help. If Joan and I decide to sell it, I need to think about what to do with the proceeds. Since we don't have kids, we want to design a trust to distribute our assets to others after we're gone. I would like to find a third trustee to work with Joan and me during our lifetimes and to administer the trust after we've passed. Our attorney is close to our ages, so I'd like to appoint another trustee who is much younger. I'm wondering if you would consider being the third trustee of the Staley Family Trust. I think you're a smart, capable person, and I believe you'd do a great job of managing the trust after we're gone. We're just starting to discuss what all this involves. You would, of course, be compensated for your time and work on behalf of the trust. And we'll have to draw up some directives for how the money would be distributed, both during our lives and after we've passed away, if the scroll were sold."

"Well, I'm honored that you'd like me to become a trustee," Matt said.

"You've mentioned that you inherited an investment account from your parents, and I need someone who's interested in and knows something about investments. If we decide to sell the scroll, there will be some money to invest. Also, I'm looking for someone with good judgment, and I've watched the way you've conducted yourself at Hacienda over the past year. I believe you would be a great teammate on our trust. You certainly don't have to give me an answer today. Take a few days to think about it. If you'd be interested in learning more about the role of a trustee, you could speak to our attorney in downtown Oakland. I'm not a trust expert, and this kind of stuff is all new to me as well."

"Yes, I'd like to think about it for a few days," Matt said, "and discuss the matter with Jancy. I'd also like to speak with your attorney as soon as it can be arranged. Could we revisit this subject in a week or two?"

"Sure. There's no hurry . . . well, not yet," Staley said, smiling. "I'd like to have a trust drawn up by Thanksgiving, and that gives us plenty of time for further discussions. I'm pleased that you're interested in exploring the possibility. I'll call our attorney, Jim Ferguson, and ask when he can speak with you. This is enough conversation about the trust. Let's call it a day, shall we?"

Matt returned to his upstairs office. In recent months, the pace of Matt's life had increased and involved taking on more responsibilities. Following his seminary graduation in May, he had obtained his first full-time job when he had been hired as an assistant minister at Hacienda Presbyterian. He'd married Jancy Nichols in June, and today, just two months later, he'd been asked by Pastor Staley to help oversee the asset of a trust that might be worth more than a million dollars. The next year would be busy, but he promised himself that, despite his new responsibilities, his marriage to Jancy would be his number one priority.

He thought about a comment Jancy had made over breakfast. *Now that Jim and Joan Staley own a Dead Sea Scroll, could their lives be in danger?*

# 2

I T HAD BEEN A WEEK since the blockbuster article about Pastor Staley's inheritance appeared in the *East Bay Times* and spread over the globe in newspapers, on the internet, across social media, and through #EstherScroll. Matt was quite sure the atmosphere at Hacienda Presbyterian would never be the same, now that its senior minister, Reverend James Staley, owned a Dead Sea Scroll. Overnight, Pastor Staley had become the most prominent clergyman in Northern California. Hacienda Presbyterian, in the affluent East Bay community of San Lucas, would forever be associated with the valuable Esther Scroll. This kind of attention would certainly elevate Hacienda's standing among the almost seventy churches that composed the Presbytery of San Francisco. This was the new reality for Matt as he stopped by the church office for a cup of coffee to start his day.

"How did last week go for you?" Matt asked Mrs. Kirby, who stood at the counter, watering a small house plant. He was impressed by her attention to such details, including her own apparel. Today, she wore a contemporary outfit that included white slacks and a peach-colored jacket, complemented by a traditional pearl necklace. "Every time I came in to check my box," he said, "you were on the phone."

Mrs. Kirby believed in loyalty. After working for Pastor Staley for seven years at his last ministry in La Jolla, she had followed him to Hacienda when he became the senior pastor ten years ago. Skeptical about Matt's commitment to his work at Hacienda, she had given him a chilly reception when he had arrived as an intern the previous year. However, after Matt survived three attempts on his life and helped Oakland Detective Ben Miller arrest church members Sally and Larry Rowland, her feelings toward Matt thawed, and she had become a good friend. The event that may have tipped the scales in Matt's favor occurred one morning, early in his internship, when he found her transferring folders from an old filing cabinet to a new one. He offered to help and completed the task in twenty minutes, whereas it would have taken Mrs. Kirby a couple of hours. She confessed that the arthritis in her back made lifting a painful activity, and she was grateful that he had spared her considerable discomfort.

"It may have been the busiest week I've had at Hacienda," she said. "Especially the phones!"

"Because of the scroll?"

"Most definitely." She looked beyond Matt through the glass window in the office door to see if anyone was about to enter. "The media wanting information, television stations like KGO and KPIX in San Francisco seeking interviews with Pastor Staley, and institutions expressing an interest in learning more about the scroll. Quite frankly, it's been a zoo around here!"

"It will be interesting to see how Pastor Staley handles all the requests," Matt said. "I don't think he wants to become a household name."

"He's receiving a ton of correspondence, too. I'm going to be very busy trying to answer all the letters. We need to write a press release and a white paper to address some of the often-asked questions."

"I'll speak to him about getting some additional office help for you, at least until things settle down."

"I'd appreciate that. I'm a little overwhelmed by it all."

"Pastor Staley seemed uncomfortable at the Sunday service when he spoke to the congregation about his inheritance. I think he feels swamped, as well," Matt commented. "Apart from the office craziness, how are you doing? Did you have a relaxing day off yesterday?"

"Very much, thank you. I curled up with a book and didn't even turn on TV!"

"Good for you! We need to be able to leave our work behind and not take it home with us. I must get ready for a meeting, so I'll see you later." Matt didn't tell Mrs. Kirby what had happened on his way to the church.

That morning, Matt had arranged to visit the San Lucas home of a new church family with a son in the high school youth group. Matt wanted to introduce himself and welcome them to Hacienda in person and leave a high school roster. He recognized that their home was located about two blocks away from the Staleys' residence on San Pedro Street. Following a brief conversation with the family in their living room, Matt returned to his car to head to Hacienda. Approaching the Staleys' house, he saw two police cars parked in front. *What's the problem?* Matt wondered as he pulled in behind the second police car.

Matt saw a dented front right fender on the second car. In the *East Bay Times* that morning, he had read about a chase the San Lucas police had two nights before with a youth from Oakland who had stolen a car near the village. The car had been parked on a residential street and wasn't locked. The police had blocked the exit from San Lucas and prevented the youth from escaping. Matt guessed that the police car may have been damaged during the incident. He walked quickly to the front steps and climbed the stairs to the porch, where he saw an open front door. Jim and Joan Staley were standing just inside, speaking to two San Lucas policemen.

"Hello, Matt," Pastor Staley said. "Come in. We had a break-in this morning, about a half-hour ago. I was at church, and Joan had driven to Hayward on an errand. We didn't activate our alarm system because we never expected something like this to happen during the day. The intruder entered through the back door."

Pastor Staley introduced Matt to the two San Lucas police officers, who had just arrived. One was an older man, Captain Wayne Meyer, stocky and slightly overweight. He wore a baseball cap with a San Lucas police emblem on it. The other officer, a younger man, introduced himself as Sergeant Ryan Richards. In his early thirties, he had a full head of dark-brown hair, along with a small tattoo of the American flag on his right forearm.

"Pastor, most of the time, break-ins involve kids who live in the neighborhood. Are there any neighbor kids you think might want to break into your home?" Captain Meyer asked.

"There aren't many kids in our neighborhood these days," Mrs. Staley said. "They've all grown up and left. We've been here for ten years, and when we arrived, there were quite a few kids. Neighborhoods have life cycles, and ours has seen an exodus of teenagers. I suppose that trend will change one of these years."

"Just the opposite is happening in my neighborhood in Livermore," Sergeant Richards said. "When we moved into our house, there were hardly any kids. Now, the place is full of them."

"We aren't aware of any kids in the immediate neighborhood who would do this," Pastor Staley said. "There's a kid who delivers our morning newspaper, but I've never met him."

"These break-ins usually involve teenage boys looking for

money or jewelry, computers and TVs to sell to buy drugs," Captain Meyer said. "Was anything stolen?"

"He took a handgun from the nightstand on my side of the bed," Pastor Staley said.

"Other than that, we don't think anything important was taken," Mrs. Staley said, "but we need to do a careful investigation. At the same time, our bedroom and office were thoroughly searched. Maybe I should say ransacked! Our bed was piled high with clothes from our bedroom closet. He must have done that in order to see what was in the rest of the closet. In our office, all the desk drawers were pulled out, so he looked in that room as well. We don't think anything other than the gun is missing from those two rooms. He must not have been here very long, and maybe he left when he heard me open the garage door."

"This break-in is especially stressful," Pastor Staley said, "because we recently inherited an ancient biblical document estimated to be worth more than a million dollars. We were wondering if this is related to our inheritance."

"That's a possibility," Captain Meyer said.

"If he left through the door to your deck," Matt said, "he might have had to climb your fence. Maybe one of your neighbors saw him."

"How well do you know your neighbors?" Captain Meyer asked.

"Fairly well," Pastor Staley said. "We haven't had much turnover on our block in the time we've lived here."

"We'll speak to a few of your neighbors," Captain Meyer said, "to learn if anyone saw something. We don't have many robberies in San Lucas, but we have a few. We'll let you know what we learn. Before I leave, I'll walk around your backyard."

"We need to get both of your fingerprints," Sergeant Richard said.

"Ours? Why?" Mrs. Staley asked.

"Yes, we need to know whose fingerprints to ignore," Sergeant Richard said. "So I'll go grab my fingerprint pad and case of powders and be back in a second. Then I'll sprinkle some dust."

"Did you say 'sprinkle dust'?" Mrs. Staley asked.

"Yes," the younger officer said. "For fingerprints. I find that graphite is the most effective. The dust sticks to the oils on the finger pads and highlights the pattern of ridges unique to each person's particular fingerprint. Then I place clear tape over the dust outlines. When I pull it up, the powdered fingerprint is transferred to the tape. It's a little like looking for a needle in a haystack, but we've arrested a few people based on their fingerprints, so I think it's worth it."

"Be my guest," Mrs. Staley said. "I'm not going anywhere the rest of the day."

"It won't take long," he said.

"I hope you have some success."

"So do I. Since you think he came in through the back door, I may start by doing some dusting on the doorknob and the glass on the French doors."

"Okay," Mrs. Staley said. "We'll let you know if we find that something else has been taken."

"Good," Captain Meyer said. "I'll have my partner collect the information about your gun, and we'll follow up with you in a day or so. I'm sorry this happened to you, but it could have been worse. I'm glad you didn't find the intruder in the house when you returned."

"Thanks for your prompt response," Pastor Staley said. "We've felt very safe here in San Lucas."

Captain Meyer told his partner he would meet him back at the police station after he checked the backyard and spoke to the neighbors. Sergeant Richards walked down the front steps and returned to the dented police car at the curb to retrieve his cache of powders.

"When I was around ten," Matt said, facing the Staleys, "my parents and I came home on New Year's Eve and found that a thief had been in our house. He had broken a basement window to gain entry. Drawers were removed from my parents' bedroom dresser, and the contents had been dumped on their bed. It was a mess. Knowing that someone has targeted and burglarized your house is not a good feeling. I hope the police can find who did it."

"Fortunately, we don't think anything valuable was taken, except for the gun." Pastor Staley said.

"That's good to hear," Matt said. "I'll be on my way."

"Thanks for your concern, Matt," Pastor Staley said. "What brings you to our neighborhood?"

"I stopped at the Callahans' home to introduce myself and leave a high school roster."

"Very good," Pastor Staley said. "I'll see you later at church."

Matt returned to his car and sat in it for a few minutes. The neighborhood was very quiet. There were no kids playing in the street, perhaps confirming that most of the kids had grown up and moved away. He didn't see any cars, either. According to city regulations, no cars could be left at the curb overnight. They had to be parked in the garage or on the driveway. Matt noticed a woman standing across the street, a few houses away, holding a yellow Lab on a leash. She was looking at the Staleys' house. Wearing slacks and a blazer, she seemed overdressed for a sunny day in August.

Later that day, Matt visited Pastor Staley's office to discuss the break-in with him.

"As I drove away," Matt said, "I noticed a woman standing across the street with a yellow Lab."

"I'm not aware there's a yellow Lab in our neighborhood. Maybe she's a new neighbor."

"Okay," Matt said.

"I rarely see a stranger on our block. Solicitors need a badge from the city to knock on doors in San Lucas. I can't recall seeing anyone I haven't known."

"Have there been any recent break-ins in your immediate neighborhood?" Matt asked.

"Not to my knowledge," Pastor Staley responded. "It's a question I should have asked the police this morning. I'll try to remember to ask them. The intruder was probably a boy from the neighborhood, and I'm concerned he took my handgun. We may never learn who it was."

"One other thing," Matt said. "Mrs. Kirby appears to be swamped with calls and correspondence about the Esther Scroll. She sounds like she could use a little help in the office, at least for a while. The phones have been ringing off the hook, not to mention all the letters."

"That's a good idea, Matt. I'll speak to David Marshall, chair of the Administration Committee, about hiring a part-time person. I've been thinking that Mrs. Kirby needs an assistant, maybe even on a full-time basis, so I'll look into it."

Pleased that Staley appeared receptive to finding some help for Mrs. Kirby, Matt returned to his office. Sitting at his desk, he wondered if the morning intruder at the Staleys' home was a neighbor kid or a professional thief. *Had the prowler been looking for the Esther Scroll?*

# 3

M ATT NOTICED THAT ACTIVITY at Hacienda Presbyterian had increased since Pastor Staley's inheritance had been reported a little over a week ago. Traffic in the church office grew with more visitors coming and going, and members started calling him for office appointments to discuss the scroll. Mrs. Kirby also sent him phone calls from members who had questions.

He reviewed Staley's invitation to become a trustee with Jancy, who endorsed the idea. They both realized he was making a long-term commitment to help Jim and Joan Staley with their future finances. Matt also believed his association with a Dead Sea Scroll would enhance his biblical knowledge, broaden his business skills, and improve his understanding of trusts and estate planning.

Another conversation he had with Jancy involved the break-in at the Staleys' home. He shared his concern that the thief may not have been a teenager from the neighborhood, but someone looking for the Esther Scroll. Both Matt and Jancy agreed that being associated with the biblical treasure may have some risks.

An appointment had been scheduled for Matt to meet with the Staleys' attorney, which was on a Thursday, two days after the break-in. The attorney's office was in the Kaiser Center in downtown Oakland, a building with which Matt was familiar.

It had been five months since he had last visited the Kaiser Center. In March, he had taken his tax return information to his CPA on the tenth floor. Today, he was visiting the seventeenth floor to meet with James Ferguson, the attorney who was setting up a trust for the Staleys.

Entering the Kaiser Center lobby, Matt was surprised again by its austere appearance. Expansive white walls contrasted with walnut paneling framing the elevator bays. A few abstract paintings, in gray and pale-blue hues, dotted the walls and added little to the visual experience. He saw a modern chandelier, consisting of slender lights hanging on cords from the ceiling, looking like a cluster of icicles. Its suggestion of winter amplified the lobby's cool and impersonal atmosphere.

Matt walked to the bank of elevators tucked into the side of the lobby. He remembered the eerie blue lighting behind the floor-selection panel. Moments after he pushed the button, the door opened, and he was grateful to be able to leave the sterile lobby.

Reaching the seventeenth floor, Matt found his way to the law offices of Hannon & MacGregor. His watch read ten forty-five. A young woman, sitting behind a long reception counter, greeted him with a cheerful smile.

"I have an eleven o'clock appointment with Mr. Ferguson," Matt said.

"I'll tell him you're here," she replied.

He turned and found a seat on a sofa against the wall, in front of a low table full of newspapers and magazines. Because he was early, he pulled out the folded *New York Times* crossword puzzle from his inside blazer pocket. Matt made considerable progress on the puzzle because Ferguson didn't appear until eleven twenty. He was setting the puzzle down to take a break when a slender man of medium height approached him, wearing a tan sport coat, a blue, button-down shirt with no tie, and brown slacks.

"Hello, Mr. Beringer," the man said. "I'm Jim Ferguson. Follow me to my office, and let's have a conversation."

"Very good," Matt replied.

Matt walked behind the attorney down a hallway to a large outer office overlooking Lake Merritt. Ferguson's desk was close to the tall windows and perpendicular to them, giving the attorney and his visitors a bird's-eye view. As Matt sat down facing Ferguson on the other side of the desk, he glanced to his left and saw a spectacular panorama of Lake Merritt below and the surrounding buildings. He recalled an evening during the previous summer when he and Jancy had taken an enjoyable walk around the lake on the three-mile path, outlined by a necklace of small lights.

"Pastor Staley has asked you if you would be interested in becoming a trustee of the Staley Family Trust," Ferguson said, "and he wants me to give you an overview of what that might involve. Is that your understanding of why you're here?"

"That's right," Matt said. "I don't have a clue as to what the responsibilities of a trustee might be. I recently graduated from Calvin Seminary, and I have to say that an understanding of legal matters isn't my strong suit."

"I'll try to improve your knowledge of trusts, at least, before you leave," he replied.

"Before you start," Matt said, never shy about asking questions, "could you tell me a little about yourself?"

"Sure. I grew up in Southern California and attended Pomona College, followed by USC Law School. I married a gal from Berkeley, so that's how I ended up in Oakland. Her parents still live in the house where she grew up. My main legal focus is wills and trusts."

"When did you start working with the Staleys?"

"That's an interesting story. I met Jim at an antique car show in Jack London Square several years ago. We were both admiring a 1930 Duesenberg Model J. We started a conversation because we both appreciate old cars, and the rest, you might say, is history. I wish I could afford to own one of those puppies, but they sell for over a million dollars! I'm in the process of trying to restore a '42 Packard in my home garage, but that's a more modest project."

"Has Pastor Staley told you what he wants to do with the Esther Scroll?"

"No," Ferguson said. "We haven't spoken that much about the future. Jim is sixty, and this inheritance may have accelerated his retirement plans, although he's told me he wants to continue working until he's sixty-five. Selling the scroll at some point would probably be the most advantageous strategy. Until then, you wouldn't have much to do as a trustee, but you'd be involved in investing the trust's assets responsibly, once the scroll is sold. That would probably involve hiring a bank trust department or finding a professional money manager. You'd want to invest the trust's assets using what is called the prudent-person rule."

"I haven't heard that term before."

"It's a guide for someone managing assets of value for other people. The rule is commonly followed by trustees and guardians given the job of administering assets on behalf of other persons. A financial manager should stay away from questionable, high-risk investments, such as penny stocks and junk bonds. Also, investments that would benefit the manager or some third party should be avoided. The prudent-person rule is a legal principle used to restrict the selections of a financial manager to the kinds of investments that an individual seeking reasonable income and preservation of capital might choose for his or her own portfolio. You'd need to think about how the investments would serve the Staleys, after Jim retires, over the following twenty or more years. If you decide to become a trustee, I suggest you take an investment course in the next year or two. You'd need to oversee the investment manager and his performance. Do you have any investment experience?"

"My parents left me a portfolio of about twenty stocks when they died not long ago," Matt said, "so I follow the stock market and the stocks we own. I also enjoy researching publicly traded companies to consider as possible future investments."

"That's good to hear," Ferguson said. "I'm a terrible stock picker, so I let someone else handle those investments for me. Do you work with a CPA?"

"Yes. Elliott James on the tenth floor, as a matter of fact."

"We might choose Elliott to work with the trust. He and I are neighbors in Piedmont. A trustee must be able to track all income, distributions, and expenditures related to the trust. This information must be distributed annually to the beneficiaries. There will be taxes to pay and tax returns to be filed. You should try to do as much as possible as a trustee, but you can hire advisors, accountants, and attorneys if you believe their assistance is in the best interest of the trust. I would strongly recommend hiring a CPA, like Elliott."

Matt glanced at the bookshelves behind Ferguson and saw some framed photos. One featured him and a woman, likely his wife, sitting under an umbrella, enjoying a drink, wearing colorful clothes. *Maybe a vacation in Hawaii.* Another photo showed Ferguson standing beside an antique car of some sort. There was a photo of the attorney holding the tiller of a large sailboat on a sunny day. *Perhaps an outing on San Francisco Bay.* "I see you're a golfer," Matt said, looking at a photo of Ferguson holding a golf club. "Is that the clubhouse behind you?"

"Yes, it's the clubhouse at Augusta National. I attend the Masters Tournament every April. That event is golf at its very finest. Two years ago, I arranged to play a round of eighteen holes. The photo was taken right after I'd finished. Quite an experience."

"I also see you standing on a red carpet," Matt said. "Where was that photo taken?"

"At the Cannes Film Festival. I like movies, and I try to attend the festival as often as possible. I even invested in a Hollywood film last year, and I may make another investment this year."

"You mentioned that you live in Piedmont," Matt said. "I know a little about Piedmont. My family's minister in Seattle was a youth leader at the Piedmont Community Church for three years while he attended Calvin Seminary in San Francisco. Do you attend that church, by chance?"

"No, my wife and I aren't attending a church right now."

"Our minister has wonderful memories of working there," Matt said. "The members were very welcoming to him. They'd invite him to dinner in their homes, which he really appreciated as a single guy because he wasn't very skillful in the kitchen. He said one couple, who lived across the street from the church, would invite him over to have a gin and tonic with them."

"I'm glad he had a good experience," Ferguson said. "We've lived in Piedmont for several years, but we haven't had time to make many friends because my wife and I both work fairly long hours."

"Our minister said he enjoyed taking his middle school group to a large camp owned by the church. It was about a three-hour drive to the camp, he said, located in Calaveras County, not far from Angel's Camp."

"You're speaking about the camp the church used to own," Ferguson said. "They sold it many years ago. My wife and I have been to the Calaveras County Fairgrounds in May to see the frog-jumping competition. It's the longest-running county fair in California."

"As I recall," Matt said, "Mark Twain wrote a short story about the jumping frogs of Calaveras County that started it."

"Yes, I think you're right. The contests began in the 1920s," Ferguson said.

"My wife and I will have to plan to see the competition next May," Matt responded.

"Those suckers can really jump," Ferguson said. "Each contestant's frog is given three jumps. The record is something like twenty-one feet. Those frogs can jump five to six feet or more! Really amazing."

"Very interesting. Do many people attend the competition?"

"It's a four-day fair," Ferguson said, "and over thirty thousand people attend each year from all over the world. The winning frogs usually have what are called frog jockeys, who rub the frogs' back legs together, drop them a short distance to the ground, and then crouch and yell at or blow on the frogs to urge them to jump. I don't know whether the frogs are frightened, but the frog jockeys usually get the best results."

*Sounds a bit cruel,* Matt thought. "Do you enjoy living in Piedmont?"

"Yes," Ferguson said. "It's quiet and safe and very convenient to the Kaiser Center."

"It sounds similar to San Lucas."

"Piedmont has an impressive history as a place where business leaders live. The Ghirardelli family, which put San Francisco chocolate on the map, built a fabulous home right in the center of Piedmont in the early 1900s. Jean Witter, one of the founders of the West Coast investment firm of Dean Witter, which later became Morgan Stanley, lived in Piedmont with his family. The Bechtel family, which founded the largest engineering firm in the US, also lived there. When San Francisco was the headquarters of the Bank of America, before being acquired by NationsBank in the late 1990s, the CEO lived in Piedmont. It's a very classy community, I'd say."

"Did you hear that the Staleys had a break-in?" Matt asked.

"Yes, Jim mentioned it to me," Ferguson said. "Probably a neighbor kid looking for drug money."

"Except for the gun, it sounds as if nothing valuable was taken," Matt said.

"Yes, they were fortunate in that respect," Ferguson said. "Well, I think we've covered enough ground in our first meeting. Are you thinking about accepting Jim's invitation to become a trustee?"

"Yes," Matt said. "Based on the duties you described, I believe I can do the job."

"I know Jim and Joan will be pleased to hear that. We should meet again in a few weeks and discuss the Staleys' goals. Thanks for coming into the office today, and I look forward to working with you. The receptionist will validate your parking."

Both Matt and Ferguson rose at the same time, shook hands, and walked together to the reception area, where Matt had his parking ticket validated and headed for the elevators. He was surprised at how short their meeting had been. Ferguson had asked him only one question about his background and qualifications. Matt had spent more time in the reception area than in Ferguson's office. However, he had learned something new about Pastor Staley. He had an interest in antique cars.

The next day, Matt called Pastor Staley to report on his meeting with Ferguson. When Staley asked him if he'd decided to become a trustee, Matt told him that he'd like to accept the position. He mentioned that he had additional questions for the attorney and planned to schedule another meeting with him.

# 4

WITHIN A WEEK OF THEIR FIRST MEETING, Matt returned to Ferguson's office to discuss the Staley Family Trust. He brought along a new list of operational and policy questions he had generated about the scroll. After checking in with the receptionist at Hannon & MacGregor, Matt walked over to a sofa in the reception area and found a seat at one end.

In a nearby chair sat a gray-haired man reading the *Wall Street Journal*. After a few minutes, the man put down the newspaper, and turned toward Matt. "Do you play for the Oakland A's?"

"No, unfortunately, I don't," Matt said with a smile.

"You look like an athlete, and I'm aware that this firm represents quite a few professional baseball players. How tall are you?"

"Six five. Are you an A's fan?" Matt asked.

"Let's say I'm an avid sports fan," he said, "including of the A's."

"I've played some sports, mainly basketball," Matt said. "How about you?"

"I was a yo-yo champion," he said, grinning.

"Really? That's interesting. I've never owned one, let alone spun one," Matt said. "I'd enjoy hearing more."

"The yo-yo has a fascinating history, going back to 500 BC in Greece. The wooden yo-yo was introduced in the United States from the Philippines in the 1920s, and by the mid-twentieth century, the toy had become a national pastime. Now most of them are plastic."

"Wow, I didn't know it's that old," Matt said.

"The yo-yo became very popular in the 1940s and 1950s because the Duncan Yo-Yo Company produced thousands of them. It became the second best-selling toy in history."

"What's number one?" Matt asked.

"The Barbie doll."

"Until the smart phone came along and took over," Matt said, smiling. "How did you become a yo-yo champion?"

"The competitions are held up in Chico, at the National Yo-Yo Museum. For several years, I'd practice three to four hours a day. When I competed, you had to perform a series of tricks, according to an established list, and the winner was the contestant who could do them all without a mistake."

"I'm glad it was an enjoyable hobby for you. It sounds like you were very good at it. Thanks for telling me about the yo-yo."

The older man smiled and returned to reading the newspaper. Matt retrieved his *New York Times* crossword puzzle from his inside blazer pocket and started working on it. After twenty minutes, Ferguson appeared, and Matt followed him to his office.

Matt had a list of topics he wanted to cover: (1) selecting an insurance company to insure the scroll, (2) choosing the safest place to preserve and store it, and (3) developing policies and procedures for handling the scroll, such as how and when it could be removed from the safe-deposit box and transported to another location. Ferguson took notes and suggested they meet with the

Staleys the following week to draft some guidelines. Matt learned that the scroll had been placed in a safe-deposit box at the East Bay headquarters of the Bank of America. Ferguson told him the Staleys wanted to add his name to the account.

Matt said he thought they should do some research into how ancient documents are stored. He had heard that a climate-controlled storage facility might be a better home for a fragile artifact than a safe-deposit box at a bank.

"It appears you've been giving considerable thought to how we take care of the Esther Scroll," Ferguson said. "We'll be sure to cover these subjects at our next meeting."

"Thanks," Matt replied. "I'm trying to help the team."

"Jim's inheritance of the Esther Scroll is a monumental event, when you think about it," Ferguson said, "both from the Staleys' financial perspective and as an archaeological discovery."

"I agree," Matt said. "These are exciting times for the Staleys and the congregation."

"Is there anything else you'd like to discuss?" Ferguson asked.

"At our last meeting, we talked about Piedmont. I have another question for you."

"Okay."

"Our minister told a story from his time at the Piedmont Community Church that made an impression on me. He said that because it's an enclosed community, surrounded by Oakland, the kids faced some social issues that were magnified because of the community's small size—there are only eleven thousand residents. For example, he said there was a social stigma assigned to kids if they lived in lower Piedmont rather than upper Piedmont, which is a similar problem kids face today in San Lucas. The question in San Lucas is, 'Do you live above the village or below it?' It seems like a ridiculous question to me. I dislike having kids defined by where they live. Do these social pressures still exist in Piedmont?"

"I don't have kids," Ferguson said, "so I'm not an expert on that subject, but I don't think those terms are used today in Piedmont. I've heard the term 'Baja Piedmont' used once or twice in jest, but whether you live above or below Highland Avenue is rarely mentioned. In my opinion, a more important measure of social status would be if you belonged to the nearby Claremont Country Club. Now that puts you in the Piedmont upper crust."

"Another attitude in San Lucas, and I wonder if it's the same in Piedmont, is the kids find life boring compared to what they think awaits them beyond the town's boundaries. The irony, in my opinion, is that the grass in San Lucas is about as green as the kids will find. After they leave San Lucas, I believe they'll soon realize what a good life they had there. Do the kids in Piedmont feel the same way?"

"Again, I'm not an expert on what kids think in Piedmont. However, from what I can see, I would tend to agree with you. The kids live in a bubble, isolated from the real world of crime and poverty. They have many advantages, including living in s safe community and attending a school with a focus on preparing them to attend college. The social pressures may not allow everyone to thrive there, but the kids may later realize the benefits of having lived in a small, affluent community."

At the end of their conversation, Ferguson said he had a colleague, George Wall, who was interested in meeting Matt because of an interest in the Dead Sea Scrolls and Pastor Staley's inheritance. Matt said he could stay longer, so Ferguson placed a call to Wall, inviting him to join them. In a matter of minutes, there was a knock on the door.

"Come in, George," Ferguson said.

The man entered the office, wearing a light-blue short-sleeve shirt and pale-green tie. "Hi, Jim. This must be Matt Beringer."

"Yes, it is," Ferguson said. "Matt, I'd like you to meet George Wall."

SECRET MOTIVES | 33

Matt stood up to shake Wall's hand. He thought Wall might be a couple of inches over six feet.

"It's good to meet you," Wall said. "Jim tells me you work with Reverend Staley at Hacienda Presbyterian in San Lucas."

"That's right," Matt said.

"My wife and I live with our two kids in Milpitas, just south of you. My wife has been hearing good things about the San Lucas school district, and she thinks we should consider moving there."

"My wife and I have an apartment in San Leandro," Matt said, "but I think San Lucas would be an enjoyable place to live."

"I was amazed when I read the article in the newspaper about the Esther Scroll," Wall said, "because I belong to the Esther Society."

Wall's comment caught Matt off guard. "The Esther Society? That's a new one on me. I haven't heard of it."

"Most people haven't heard about it," Wall said, "and that's fine with us. We're not seeking publicity and prefer to fly under the radar screen. We're a global organization of about two thousand members, Christians and Jews, who promote the Ten Commandments. The organization was started about twenty years ago because the founders believed the Ten Commandments deserve more recognition than they were receiving. Just as Esther in the Old Testament rescued the Jewish people, we don't want the world to forget about the Ten Commandments. They're the basis of our legal system here in the United States."

"I'd say the Ten Commandments are fairly well-known, wouldn't you?" Matt asked.

"Twenty or thirty years ago, I might have agreed with you. Today, we believe their influence is slowly being eroded in the United States, where the church has been pushed out of the town square by the courts, opponents, and non-believers. In some parts of the world, such as in South Korea, Christianity is growing, but we're concerned about a declining focus on our Judeo-Christian values and the Ten Commandments in the United States and Europe. We're trying to turn things around."

"I read an article," Matt said, "that asserted that until 1994, being a Christian was a social advantage. Then it became a social neutral, and in 2014, it became a social disadvantage. Some people today might say it's no longer relevant to be a Christian. I'm aware that the denominational churches in the US are losing members, and that's not a good trend. And in Europe, both Christians and Jews are being threatened and attacked, and churches and synagogues are being damaged."

"We think many people in the US have replaced God with Government, using a capital G."

"That's an interesting concept. I hope it hasn't reached that point. How does your organization promote the Ten Commandments?"

"Every year," Wall said, "we select three themes to sponsor, relating to the Ten Commandments and their values. We work with denominations and church organizations, as well as individual churches and synagogues, especially in the US and Europe, to promote these themes. We speak with the media and buy selective ads, and we communicate with elected officials and support legislation that is compatible with the Ten Commandments."

"Can you give me an example of one of your recent themes?" Matt asked.

"Okay. Let's take, for example, the Fourth Commandment: "Remember the Sabbath and keep it holy." We think the world would be a healthier place if persons paused one day a week and gave thanks to God for our many blessings. I'll drill down a little farther. It says in the Fourth Commandment that animals should not work on the Sabbath. God is demanding the humane treatment of animals. We believe that kindness toward animals is required of all people. The Bible speaks against animal suffering, and we work to promote this attitude around the world. The society is a strong financial supporter of the SPCA, the Society for the Prevention of Cruelty to Animals."

"I like that," Matt replied. "Do you have a website?"

"No," Wall said. "That's not our style. We're not interested in promoting the society."

"I'd like to learn more about your organization."

"Maybe you and I should have lunch sometime. Let me mention another commandment that is like the Fourth Commandment. All but two of the Ten Commandments are inherently negative because they say, 'You shall not.' Besides the Fourth, the other positive commandment is the Fifth, 'Honor your father and your mother.' Without going into too much detail, we believe that honoring parents is the glue that holds us together and gives our society its structure. Also, if children don't honor their parents, they're less likely to honor God. These two commandments are so important to God that they are given to us as assignments. The other commandments mainly tell us what to avoid. By supporting the Fifth Commandment, the Esther Society promotes family values and laws that help unite the family."

"Yes, I'd like to have lunch with you and hear more about the society," Matt said. "Where is your headquarters located?"

"Jackson Hole, Wyoming."

"Are most of your members in the US?" Matt asked.

"I'd say more than half are," Wall replied, "although we have members in over twenty countries. And quite a few of us are attorneys."

"Can you give me a business card?" Matt asked. "I'd like to call you in the next week."

"I look forward to it." Wall handed Matt his business card, shook his hand, and left the office.

Matt was surprised he had never heard of the Esther Society. He had attended church since he was five and spent three years at a seminary, but he had never heard about this organization. It sounded to him as if it could be some sort of secret society. *If they were promoting biblical values, why did they need to keep such a low profile?* Matt wondered.

Turning to Ferguson, Matt said, "Thanks for the introduction. I've never heard of the Esther Society, so it's interesting to learn about it. How long have you known George Wall?"

"Maybe five years," Ferguson replied. "He attended UCLA law school, so we have an annual bet on the USC-UCLA football game." It was the first time Matt had seen Ferguson smile.

"He and I have similar interests," Matt responded. "I'd like to hear more about his organization."

"I don't think he's going anywhere soon," Ferguson replied, "so you know where you can reach him."

"I look forward to meeting with you and the Staleys," Matt said.

"Yes, I'll call the Staleys and ask when they're available. I'll have my assistant call you with the day and time."

"Very good. See you soon." Matt rose and left Ferguson's office. He didn't know what to think about the Esther Society. Was it promoting the Ten Commandments, or did it have another, less obvious agenda? He looked forward to telling Jancy and Pastor Staley about it and hearing their reactions. Surely Staley knew about it. Matt was curious about why Wall was so interested in meeting him.

*Could the Esther Society have designs on the Esther Scroll?*

# 5

MATT SAT AT THE DESK in his upstairs office, staring at the five-by-seven-inch framed photo in front of him. The picture showed Jancy and him, facing the camera, standing in the wicker basket of a hot-air balloon, seconds before they lifted off for an hour-long flight over the countryside around Livermore. It was their most unusual wedding present from two months ago—a gift from the Foley family, long-time church members and enthusiastic hot-air balloonists.

It was Matt's first and probably last hot-air balloon ride. Guided by Bill Foley, the balloon rose to over one thousand feet in a matter of seconds. As someone who isn't a great fan of heights, Matt's heart became stuck in his throat. Jancy, however, loved the experience. There was very little wind that day—one of the required conditions for hot-air ballooning—so the balloon moved slowly once it reached the intended elevation. Foley kept the balloon at a height of between one and two thousand feet, and that was just fine with Matt. Below them on the ground, the Foleys' van, driven by Mrs. Foley, followed the balloon's movements. From the air, the van was just a speck. After Foley stopped firing the burner to heat the air and lift the balloon, Jancy commented about how quiet it was floating through space. Upon reaching the desired altitude, Foley opened the parachute valve, exposing the hole at the top of the envelope, thereby limiting the height of the balloon's flight. The air escaped through the parachute valve and caused the balloon to descend, which required Foley to periodically fire the burner to stay at the same elevation. Matt thought it was an exhilarating experience for both of them, even though he guessed that Jancy would be more eager than he to accept another invitation. He recalled his relief when the balloon landed, and he was able to put his feet on terra firma.

Now it was August, and Matt thought about the cloud hanging over his arrival exactly one year ago to begin his internship at Hacienda Presbyterian. A previous intern, Pete Rockwell, had died two weeks before. Initially, it was thought Rockwell had fallen asleep at the wheel of his car while returning on I-80 to his apartment in Sacramento, but weeks later, investigators decided he had been forced off the road by a semi.

A second fatality occurred shortly thereafter, involving the next intern, Richard Finley. He had tragically died the day before Matt's first day on the job. Matt had arrived at Lake Chabot to meet Finley because they were scheduled to have dinner together. However, when Matt saw Finley, an expert sailor, floating in the water beside the rented sailboat, he swam out to get him and brought him back to the dock, where paramedics tried unsuccessfully to revive him. An autopsy revealed that Finley had fallen into the water while sailing because he had been poisoned by a sandwich containing a deadly white powder used in rat poison.

Matt also became a murder target, fortunately escaping three attempts on his life. With Jancy's moral support, Matt and his friend,

Detective Ben Miller of the Oakland Police Department, identified and captured the murderer, Sally Rowland. A church leader and pillar of the community, she had organized the attempted murder of Matt, as well as the deaths of his two predecessors. In her confession, she admitted she was seeking revenge for the accidental drowning death of her son on a church canoe trip on the Russian River involving the middle school group. It has been organized by Pete Rockwell and unfortunately had also resulted in the deaths of two other youths. When Sally was arrested for murder, and her husband, Larry, was charged as an accomplice, the congregation was devastated. It shook the community that such evil deeds had been perpetrated by members of a church. Both Sally and Larry Rowland were convicted of their crimes. Sally Rowland's plot to murder three seminarians also destroyed her own family.

Even though Matt had been her third murder target, he had made a commitment to visit Sally and her husband in jail to try to help them recover their faiths. He had another visit scheduled with them in just a few days.

During his internship, Matt had met Jancy Nichols, a former Hacienda employee. Their romantic relationship flourished, and he asked her to marry him in June, following the completion of his internship and his graduation from Calvin Theological Seminary. Jancy accepted his proposal, and the entire congregation was invited to attend the celebration.

How wrong Matt had been to think that his job as an intern at Hacienda Presbyterian would be boring at times. His experience had been just the opposite. And now with Jim Staley's inheritance of the Esther Scroll, it was beginning to feel as if there might be trouble ahead. Time would tell.

Matt considered that Jim Staley's inheritance of a priceless treasure might present some new risks for him, given his new role as a trustee of the Staley Family Trust. Someone might want to steal the valuable treasure and sell it on the black market for a huge sum of money. He hoped Jancy wasn't as concerned as he was about the potential hazards. He also worried about the safety of the Staleys, and he wondered if the break-in at their home was a preview of future events.

The framed photo next to the hot-air balloon ride showed Matt in his Little League baseball uniform, sitting on the front steps of his home in Seattle. Next to him was his family's white standard poodle, Prince. He remembered when Prince had arrived at Seattle-Tacoma International Airport in a crate from a breeder in Southern California, and Matt had accompanied his parents to the airport to bring home their dog. It must have been a frightening airplane trip for the young pup, but he quickly became a member of the family. Smart, affectionate, and loyal, Prince brought great joy to the Beringer household. When his parents decided it was time to have Prince put down at age twelve due to failing health, it was one of the saddest days in Matt's life. It happened during the summer following his first year at Princeton, and the loss of Prince created a void that Matt felt for the entire summer.

Matt's mother was usually preparing dinner in the kitchen when he and his dad arrived home from the late afternoon Little League baseball games, and she could see them as they approached the house from the driveway. She said she could tell if his team had won or lost by the way he walked up the front porch steps.

His mind wandered to an experience he had as a Little Leaguer that illustrated how adults around him were not always looking out for his best interests. People, even adults in leadership positions, are not always supportive and do not treat people equally. From first-hand experience, Matt saw how people can disregard the feelings of others when they conflict with their own goals.

When he was twelve, starting his final year of Little League baseball in Seattle, his team's manager was the father of one of his teammates, all of whom he knew because they attended his elementary school. Matt was waiting for his dad to come home from work to take him to his team's practice. However, when his dad arrived, he told Matt that he wouldn't be going to practice because he had been traded to another team for some baseball equipment—bats, balls, and mitts. Matt was surprised that his manager wanted to let him go. He had never heard of player trades occurring among the teams in his league. And being traded for baseball equipment made no logical sense. Matt knew he was more valuable than baseball equipment. He didn't understand why his manager had traded him, and he and his father never discussed the matter.

Matt put the experience behind him, and a few days later his dad drove him to the first baseball practice with his new team. His teammates all attended a Catholic elementary school, not far from where Matt lived, and the manager was a member of the adjacent church. The Catholic Church was a foreign world to Matt since his parents didn't attend church and he accompanied neighbors to a nearby Presbyterian church. However, his new manager and teammates welcomed him with open arms, for which he was very grateful. Matt looked forward to helping his new team win some baseball games. That summer was one of his most enjoyable baseball seasons, and he was chosen for the league All-Star team as the center fielder. Given his All-Star selection, Matt wondered what his former manager thought about the wisdom of trading him. In any case, the experience showed Matt that decisions or events may not seem fair on the surface but later prove informative, educational, or even providential. Matt was grateful to play his last year for a manager who wanted him on the team. What began as a confusing and disappointing event in his life blossomed into a beautiful experience that seemed to have been ordained.

The mystery of Matt's trade for baseball equipment was finally solved at his fifth-year high school reunion in Seattle, which he chaired. A committee member told him that his former Little League teammate, whose dad had been the manager, had said some disparaging and untruthful words about Matt. While Matt's Little League experience didn't compare with his encounter with Sally Rowland, it was an early education he received about how a person's pride—feeling superior to others by having the power to gain control over them—can be hurtful. A Little League manager, likely encouraged by his son, had found a way to remove Matt from the team and exercised that power. And, more recently, Sally Rowland wanted her way so badly that she conspired to murder three seminary interns.

Matt's eyes moved to the third framed photo on his desk. It showed his parents, facing the camera, sitting on a large driftwood log on a beach at Hood Canal, a natural saltwater inlet to the west of Seattle and part of the larger Puget Sound. Matt remembered that day when he was fourteen as if it were yesterday. On that warm summer afternoon twelve years ago, he and his parents were visiting a family who owned a summer cabin on the canal. It was the only time he could recall that he and his parents walked on a beach together. He wished he could recapture that day and walk the beach with them again.

One of the reasons Matt changed directions and decided to attend seminary rather than business school was because he wanted to gain a better understanding of the human capacity for being good and bad. From experience, he had learned that people have the potential to inflict considerable hurt on others. Therefore, he didn't agree with the concept that people are basically good. He wanted to know why people hurt each other and how persons on the receiving end might respond to their suffering. During his seminary years, Matt became interested in the flawed human natures found in the Old Testament and how God had dealt with them. He had read about the power of forgiveness in the New Testament and how it can be life changing. His search for explanations to life's injustices and suffering had generated some answers. He learned that the conflict for a moral world is waged primarily through an inner struggle against pride, ingratitude, weakness, laziness, addiction, and evil. By his graduation, Matt believed he had gained insights into some of the questions he had brought to the seminary, but not all of them.

His eyes returned to the photo of him sitting next to Prince, which reminded him of the woman with the yellow Lab who was standing across the street from the Staleys' house after the break-in. He wondered if she was somehow connected to his meeting the day before with George Wall at James Ferguson's office.

That caused thoughts to swirl in his head—about the Esther Society, its apparent secrecy, and George Wall's interest in meeting him to discuss the Esther Scroll. Then they spun even further. *Did the Walls own a yellow Lab? Was the woman across the street George Wall's wife, monitoring the aftermath of a robbery planned and executed by the Esther Society?*

The telephone ringing on Matt's desk interrupted his stream of consciousness.

# 6

By the third week in August, the pace of life at Hacienda had slowed to a crawl with many in the congregation away on vacations. Matt's desk calendar showed he had no meetings on the third Wednesday. Even Pastor Staley decided to take a day off. Staley had arranged a getaway for Wednesday and Thursday nights at a hotel in Sausalito as a surprise for his wife, but he had forgotten about a Thursday morning car tune-up he had scheduled at Carl's Garage. He asked a favor of Matt—to take his Lincoln to the garage for the appointment. Staley said they would drive their second car to the hotel in Marin County.

Matt said he was glad to help. He would drive the Staleys' car home after work, leaving his car at the church overnight. The next morning, he would deliver their car to the garage at nine. Jancy would follow him and take him to Hacienda on her way to work.

On that Wednesday evening, Matt had a minor complication. He had agreed to attend a seven o'clock meeting at the Hayward

YMCA, so he would drive there in the Staleys' Lincoln, before heading home.

Matt had told Jancy that he would work late, grab a McDonald's hamburger and milkshake on the way to the Y, and be home by around eight thirty. It was an organizational session for the men's basketball program at the Y that ran from October to March. The previous year, he had played on the team that had won the league championship. Having games twice a week was good exercise, and he looked forward to resuming competition. Basketball had moved down three or four notches on his list of priorities since his days of playing on the Princeton varsity team, and he welcomed the more relaxed atmosphere at the Hayward Y.

After finding a parking spot for the Staleys' car a couple of blocks from the Y, Matt walked toward the building's entrance. His thoughts were distracted by the not-so-pleasant memories from the previous season when a teammate had tried to kill him, driving him off a pier and into the bay when he was a passenger in the fellow's pickup. Tom Dawson, aka Al Agnew and Sally Rowland's hire, had been a late addition to Matt's team. Agnew had been a congenial teammate during the season, and when he asked Matt if he wanted to have a beer with a few players at the Green Parrot Bar & Grill after a game, Matt accepted his invitation. Following the incident, Agnew had disappeared for a few weeks, but when the Rowlands were arrested, he resurfaced and admitted to his role in the murder plot.

As Matt entered the YMCA, he could hear the familiar sound of bouncing basketballs in the gym, located next to the lobby. A meeting sign that read "Men's Basketball League," located inside the front door, with an arrow on it, pointed Matt to the room next to the gym where the director had set up some chairs. A few of the chairs were occupied, but other young men soon followed Matt into the room, eventually numbering fifteen.

The director, Roy Waite, was standing behind a lectern. A slender, balding man of medium height in his late fifties, he had thin lines on his forehead and gray hair around his ears. Waite wore tan cords, a gray sweatshirt, and light-brown Sperry topsiders. His erect posture exuded self-confidence and authority. Matt guessed he was a former gym rat, involved in sports all his life, and destined to find a career in a field associated with athletics. With hundreds of guys coming and going at the Y, Waite greeted Matt by his first name. The ability to remember names confirmed to Matt that Waite enjoyed his work and had mastered some leadership skills. If the senior management of the Bay Area YMCAs was smart, Matt concluded, it would give Roy Waite at least one more promotion before he retired.

"Fellas, thanks for being here tonight," Waite said, starting the meeting promptly at seven. "I've organized these meetings for the past several years because they've been helpful to me. I typically invite last year's team captains and other team leaders. Here's my agenda. I want to share my hopes and goals for the fall and winter basketball program I started fourteen years ago when I came to the Hayward YMCA. I'd also like to tell you a little about myself and my experience with the Y. In addition, I plan to discuss the core values of the Y that I hope you'll include in the way you live. And finally, I'm interested in learning about potential concerns or problems before the basketball season starts, so I can deal with them before they interfere with the program."

Waite took off his watch and laid it on the lectern. "As much as I like basketball, I have bigger goals for you than just providing a place for you to shoot baskets. Growing up in Sacramento, I was a latchkey kid. Both of my parents had jobs. I didn't see them until they came home from work. Fortunately, there was a YMCA located not far from where I lived. It was my home away from home. The Y became my family, and I always felt welcome and accepted by the friendly and supportive staff. At the Y, I learned some important life values. I also learned how to play basketball, and I became good enough to earn a basketball scholarship that allowed me to attend college. I don't know what I'd be doing today if it hadn't been for the YMCA. Maybe I would have joined a street gang and ended up on drugs. Later, when I went to work for the Y, I wanted the Y to make a positive impact on as many kids as possible, just as I had experienced. I've started basketball programs at each of the three YMCAs where I've worked. Here in Hayward, our basketball program starts at age twelve. I've been especially pleased with the steady growth of our men's basketball program, for ages twenty to forty, and I'm looking forward to another successful year."

Reaching for a portable bulletin board he had brought to the meeting, Waite pulled it close to the lectern. Pointing to the bulletin board, he continued, "Here's a poster with the core values of the YMCA. I'd like to read them to you. These are the values that I learned about at the Y, that changed my life in a positive way, and that I hope you will incorporate into your lives. Caring—showing a concern for others. Honesty—be truthful in what you say and what you do. Respect—treat others the way you want to be treated. Responsibility—be accountable for your promises and actions. Inclusion—accept, welcome, and embrace all."

Matt recalled that Waite had discussed these core values at a similar meeting a year ago, only this year, after reading them, he used new stories to illustrate each one of them.

Waite spoke from the heart and drew from his own experiences at the Y to convey why he believed the values are so important. He concluded his comments by saying, "I'd like you to include the YMCA's core values in the way you live because I believe they'll make you a better person."

The third value Waite discussed was especially meaningful to Matt. The Golden Rule, found in Matthew 7:12, says, "So in everything, do to others what you would have them do to you, for this sums up the Law and the Prophets." Matt's mother once told him it was the most important belief that guided her life. When he left the Y that evening, he would ask for a brochure listing the YMCA's core values and put it on the bulletin board in his office.

Following his remarks, Waite paused, shuffled some papers on the lectern in front of him, and then continued. "While I expect another successful basketball season, I've found it helpful to compare notes with a handful of you guys before the season begins. It gives me a chance to get a reading on what you're thinking and try to resolve any problems that exist. Do any of you have questions or concerns about the basketball program?"

A man in the second row raised his hand. "This isn't super-important, Mr. Waite, but I'd like to see the Y install a few more vending machines with beverages, energy bars, and snack foods. I'm usually thirsty and hungry after the games, and it would be great to be able to buy something here at the Y instead of having to stop at a store on my way home."

"I think that's a good suggestion, and I'll look into it and see what I can do," Waite responded. "I'll get back to you after I do some research. Let me have a show of hands if the rest of you agree with his suggestion."

Almost all the men raised their hands.

Another young man stood up and said, "Could the Y open for a few hours on Sunday, so I could practice shooting on my day off? I own my own business and often work six days a week. During some weeks, Sunday is the only day I have off."

"I wish we could keep the Y open seven days a week, but we have a limited budget, and I can't afford to staff this place on Sundays. Maybe someday we'll be able to expand our hours, but we just aren't able to do it right now. I'm sorry about that."

Another hand was raised. "Will any teams from last year remain intact or will all of the rosters be different?"

"All the teams will have totally different rosters," Waite said.

"I'm surprised at how evenly matched the teams are," another man said. "How do you do it?"

"Well, I've been putting the teams together for quite a few years now," Waite said. "You may remember that the form you completed, when you signed up, asked for information about your height and weight and basketball experience. You were asked if you played on a high school or college team and so forth. That helps me balance the talent. You also gave me your phone number, so if I want to know more about your basketball history, I can give you a call. Is there anything else you'd like to discuss tonight?"

His question was met with silence.

"Well, gentlemen, our conversation has been very helpful," Waite said. "Also, I'm glad it's been a short meeting." He laughed. "My wife will be surprised to see me arrive home so early this evening. I've mailed 150 postcards to the men who participated in our basketball program last year, and based on RSVPs, I think we'll be able to organize two leagues again this year, six teams in each, with about ten players on each team. I received a couple of complaints last year from men who said their teams favored playing the best players over giving everyone equal time on the court. And I need to remind you that, besides being a place for exercise, I have important objectives for our basketball program: to encourage good sportsmanship, to promote friendship formation, to give everyone equal playing time, and to put these goals above winning ball games." Waite surveyed the men in the room and smiled. "Again, thanks for coming tonight, and I'll see you in early October."

It was seven thirty when Matt strolled out of the Y and headed to his car. The evening was warm, but a light breeze blowing in from the bay softened the heat. The meeting had been a good start to the approaching basketball season. He liked Roy Waite's honesty and openness. Matt looked forward to playing basketball again and wondered who Waite would put on his team.

There wasn't much traffic in downtown Hayward. As Matt walked toward the car, he noticed a man standing on the sidewalk, peering into the passenger's window. He was wearing jeans and a dark jacket but was too far away for Matt to clearly see his face. When the man saw him approaching, he crossed the street and disappeared between two buildings. *Was that guy thinking about stealing the Staleys' car?* Matt wondered. When he reached the car, he walked around it to see if anything had been done to it. Nothing. After climbing in, Matt sat in the driver's seat for a minute and considered if he should try to trail the man. At the same time, maybe the stranger was just admiring the Lincoln. Matt put the key in the ignition and pulled away from the curb. It had been a long day, and he was ready to head home.

Matt drove on Carlos Bee Boulevard heading west, which became Orchard Avenue. Then he turned onto West Jackson Street, leading to the Nimitz Freeway. Entering the onramp to the freeway heading north to Oakland, he was just minutes from the Davis Street exit leading to his apartment on Chumalia Street in San Leandro. He looked forward to seeing Jancy.

The nighttime traffic on the Nimitz was always busy. Wave after wave of cars and trucks charged north in a hurry on I-880. The artery that ran from San Jose along the East Bay to Oakland, Sacramento, and beyond never stopped pumping cars in either direction. Matt smiled as he recalled the bumper sticker that said, "Pray for Me, I Drive the Nimitz." The Nimitz had a reputation for being a dangerous stretch of highway, partly due to the many heavy trucks, banned from a parallel section of the MacArthur Freeway, crowding into this already congested route. At the top of the onramp, Matt had to slow to find an opening in the rush of vehicles heading north. Once he was able to enter the surge, he looked forward to a quick exit. He was impressed with how the Staleys' Lincoln accelerated.

Matt disliked tailgaters, and he had noticed a dark car behind him on West Jackson near the Y that had followed closely behind him. Fortunately, the car changed lanes once they entered the Nimitz, and he lost track of it. Matt stayed in the far-right lane, so he would be in a position to exit at Davis Street. Then the tailgater reappeared in his rearview mirror, one lane over. The car was accelerating and closing the distance between them. Matt hoped the driver was planning to pass him and continue on his way. However, it didn't look that way. The car seemed to be angling toward his left rear fender. Matt heard the loud thud of metal hitting metal as the older Ford sedan slammed into the Lincoln. His foot automatically stepped on the brake. Jolted by the impact, he felt the back of his car pushed to the right and realized he was losing control of his car. A surge of adrenaline rushed through him. At sixty-five miles an hour, the car made a 180-degree turn and finally skidded to a stop beside the cement bulkhead at the edge of the freeway. His brakes had slowed the speed of his spin, but he was alarmed to be facing the wrong way on a very busy freeway. The line of headlights of oncoming cars and trucks shining on him told Matt he needed to turn around quickly. Fortunately, the traffic in his far-right lane had stopped, but horns had started to blare while vehicles in the adjacent lanes continued to speed by him. Matt made a U-turn, and then he floored the Lincoln and moved forward quickly toward the Davis Street exit.

It was doubtful that anyone saw the license plate of the car that hit him, and he just wanted to get out of there. He hoped the damage to the Staleys' car was minimal.

In less than a mile, Matt took his exit and drove to his apartment on Chumalia Street. In the basement parking garage, he surveyed the Lincoln and noticed some serious scratches and a few dents on the left-rear bumper, but nothing major. He winced at the thought of having to give this news to the Staleys. More than anything, he was glad to have escaped the lunatic driver on the Nimitz Freeway, famous for its drunks, road ragers, and short-fused truck drivers at the ends of long trips. He felt a sense of relief as he took the elevator to the second floor. Matt had a story to tell Jancy that might curl her hair.

*Was the driver of the car that rammed him targeting Pastor James Staley, the new owner of the Esther Scroll?*

# 7

THE NEXT MORNING, Matt drove the Staleys' car to Carl's Garage
for the nine o'clock tune-up, with Jancy following in her car.
Matt phoned Pastor Staley from the garage to tell him about the
accident and was relieved when Staley told him not to worry about
it. Staley said they were having a good time in Sausalito and would
return the next day. Jancy took Matt to Hacienda and continued on
her way to her job in Oakland's Montclair neighborhood.

The following day, Staley visited the garage and learned that
the body work would cost several thousand dollars. He told Matt
he that he planned to file an insurance claim. Staley consoled Matt
by telling him that it could have been much worse, that he could
have been hurt, and not to fret about a few dents to their car. Matt
was sorry for the complications that the accident had added to the
Staleys' lives, but he couldn't change what had happened.

However, Matt decided it was time for him to place a call to his
friend, Detective Ben Miller of the Oakland Police Department.

"Hey, Ben, this is Matt Beringer. How are things with you?"

"It's good to hear from you. You'll be glad to know that last month Alexis and I took a two-week vacation and drove up the Oregon coast to Cannon Beach. We had a great time, and thanks for telling me all about that place. We walked the beach and had some wonderful meals. It was a very relaxing week."

"Did you visit Ecola State Park?" Matt asked.

"You bet," Ben said. "We had a couple of picnics there. It's a beautiful setting. I had the list of places to see that you gave me. Your fingerprints are all over our trip, buddy. We examined the tide pools at Haystack Rock, and we rode horses on the beach with a small group and a guide. One morning, we sculpted an alligator in the sand. A father and his young daughter, maybe four or five years old, stopped to watch us. She asked, 'Is it real?'"

"I'm really glad you had a good time," Matt said. "How was the weather?"

"The weather was fabulous! We had a couple of foggy mornings, but the afternoons were warm, clear, and sunny. I even flew a kite! Haven't done that in years. Alexis wants to move there."

"Cannon Beach rarely disappoints," Matt said. "What do you hear from your brother?"

"We've seen less of Sidney this year than last year!"

"He owes me a phone call, as well," Matt said.

"Do you know he's engaged?" Ben asked.

"Sidney?! I don't believe it."

"Yeah, we've met her and like her."

"What's Sidney doing after business school?" Matt asked. "He hasn't told me where he's working."

"He was hired by a Silicon Valley tech company. I think it's located in Sunnyvale. His fiancée works for a tech company in San Francisco. Maybe you, Jancy, Alexis, and I will have to drive to San Francisco and have dinner with them some evening. That may be the only way we'll be able to see them."

"Sounds like a plan," Matt said. "Pick a couple of dates and let me know. We'd love to join you."

"What's happening with you?" Ben asked. "How's the married man?"

"I'm really enjoying it. Marriage with Jancy is everything I hoped it would be."

"That's good to hear," Ben said. "I'm glad Alexis and I could attend your wedding. It was a very nice celebration. Your uncle Cal told me he was so proud to be your best man. I know your parents were looking down on you that day with big smiles on their faces."

"I know they were, too."

"The church was full," Ben said. "I didn't know you had that many friends."

"We invited the entire congregation," Matt said, chuckling.

"By helping to arrest the Rowlands, you became a San Lucas hero overnight! It was a great way to start your work there."

"You and I had some wild and woolly times on that case, didn't we?"

"You can say that again," Ben said. "What else is new, Reverend?"

"Well, I miss hanging out with you and catching murderers."

"Yeah, yeah," Ben said, "that's funny. So why haven't I heard from you?"

"My schedule is crazy. My supervisor hasn't given me my new job description, so I've been pretty much winging it at church. I still work with the middle school program, but I've become involved with high school kids and grade school kids, too. Also, I'm asked to give an occasional sermon. That, plus marriage, keeps me off the streets and out of trouble. Sort of . . ."

"What do you mean, sort of?" Ben asked.

"I may have a problem."

"Wait a minute! You could write a best-selling mystery novel about what happened to you last year! Now what's going on? Don't tell me you've uncovered another murder plot?"

"Maybe."

"You've got to be kidding," Ben said. "Okay, so tell me what you have."

"Did you read about Pastor Staley inheriting a Dead Sea Scroll?"

"Do I like chocolate milkshakes?! Of course, I heard about it. It was front-page news a couple of weeks ago. I even thought about calling you, but I don't fully appreciate the archaeological significance of the scroll, so I decided not to bother you."

"Besides its historical importance," Matt said, "the Esther Scroll is extremely valuable. It may be worth well over a million dollars, so Pastor and Mrs. Staley have become wealthy overnight."

"I hear you," Ben said. "I thought about that when I read the article. They may have some new security issues they didn't have before. I suspect someone leaked the information to the media because I'm sure they didn't want their inheritance to be made public."

"You're right."

"So how does this involve you?" Ben asked.

"The Staleys asked me to become a trustee of the Staley Family Trust, which includes the scroll. When they sell the scroll, I'll be overseeing the investment of the money for their retirement and other purposes."

"The plot thickens."

"Yeah," Matt said. "The Staleys just had a break-in at their house. I think it may have been someone looking for the scroll. The police think it was probably a neighborhood kid, but I saw someone who looked to be casing their home as I drove away."

"You were there right before the break-in?"

"No," Matt said. "Just by coincidence, I happened to be in the neighborhood right after the break-in. I saw two police cars in front of their house, so I stopped to see what was going on. After the police left, I went to my car to go to work, and I saw a woman across the street, looking at their house. That seemed a little odd to me."

"You have an active imagination," Ben said, "but go on."

"All I'm saying is that I think some strange things could happen because of Staley's inheritance, and I just wanted you to know how I'm involved with the scroll."

"Thanks, buddy," Ben said. "I hope the scroll is stored at a bank and not at their house."

"You're right, it is, but greedy people can do bizarre things. As a trustee, couldn't I be in some danger as well?"

"I doubt it," Ben said, "but who knows? Who would have guessed that Sally Rowland was a murderer? She was an elder at the church! Why did you volunteer for the trustee position?"

"Just trying to be helpful to the Staleys," Matt said, "but now I'm having second thoughts."

"Is this the trouble you mentioned when you called?"

"Not exactly," Matt said. "I have one more story for you."

"I can't wait."

"Last night I was coming home from a meeting at the Hayward Y," Matt said, "driving on the Nimitz at around sixty-five miles an hour, and someone rear-ended me. I did a one-eighty, ended up facing the wrong way, but fortunately I was able to turn around and drive to my exit in San Leandro. It could have been much worse. The car that hit me seemed to have been following me for several blocks before I entered the Nimitz, so I don't know if it was a random event or whether I was being targeted. The other thing, more importantly, is that I was driving the Staleys' Lincoln, so the tailgater may have been targeting Pastor Staley."

"The art of living dangerously," Ben said. "It sounds to me that you're becoming a seasoned veteran."

"I wonder if anyone reported the spin-out last night. I was kind of hoping that someone spotted it and phoned you guys."

"Probably not," Ben said, "but I'll look into it and call you if someone did."

"One other thing," Matt said. "When I walked to the car after the meeting at the Y, there was a man looking into the car. When he saw me, he walked away quickly. I wonder if he was the same guy who then followed me onto the Nimitz."

"Your guess is as good as mine," Ben said, "but it sounds like either you or the Lincoln drew a lot of attention last night. I'll have one of the detectives check to see if any traffic cameras picked up anything."

"Any words for the wise?" Matt asked.

"Last year, when you really were a murder target, I advised you to avoid evening meetings. Most of the bad stuff happens after the sun goes down, as you discovered last night."

"It's an occupational hazard. I have evening meetings at church because that's when members are available."

"Well, fortunately for you," Ben said, "San Lucas is a safe community. I'd avoid potentially dangerous places at night, like the Nimitz. Stay in touch, buddy. I'm concerned about your welfare, and I'll stay alert to anything strange that comes through the station. I want to see a little Ben Beringer running around the basketball court one day. Don't hesitate to call me again if something suspicious happens."

"Thanks. I appreciate your support," Matt said.

"Last year, you almost lost your life. I don't want to see you in that kind of danger."

"I really appreciate your concern," Matt said. "It's good to have a friend in law enforcement. Let's have lunch one of these days. I think it's my turn to buy."

"Yeah, you owe me one, now that you have a full-time job. Take care, brother. You'll be hearing from me about dinner with Sidney."

"Okay," Matt said. "I look forward to it. You take care, my friend."

# 8

It was a warm Thursday in mid-August, with the temperature in the East Bay over eighty degrees. Matt went to Pastor Boyle's office in the afternoon to discuss the senior high program. He wanted to tell Boyle about a high school group barbecue that would be held at a senior's home, hosted by the parents, which included swimming in the family's pool. As usual, Boyle received the information without asking a single question.

Boyle's indifference to the overall youth program he supervised continued, which had been Matt's experience with his supervisor the year before during his internship. Boyle wanted to be informed about what Matt was doing as leader of the middle school group, but he admitted that his heart wasn't invested in working with youth. Matt had been hired as an assistant minister to take over more of Boyle's supervisory duties and lighten his workload.

As Matt was leaving, Boyle motioned for him to return to the chair in front of his desk.

"Beringer, it's about time that you and I went to an A's game. There's a game with the Seattle Mariners this Saturday afternoon at one o'clock. I know they're your hometown team. What do you say?"

"That's sounds great! Let me check with Jancy. I'm sure she'll be okay with it. I try to keep Saturdays free to spend with her, but she knows I'm a big baseball fan."

"Should we meet at the church and ride together?" Boyle asked.

"Good idea," Matt said. "I'll drive us to the Coliseum. What time should we meet?"

"Let's make it at eleven thirty. The game starts around one o'clock, so we'll arrive with time to spare. That will give us a chance to see the teams warming up. It will be fun to see how the Mariners compete against the A's."

"The teams have similar records," Matt said, "so let's hope it's a close game."

"The weather is supposed to be sunny and warm," Boyle said.

"Let's have lunch at the game," Matt said. "I'll buy."

"You're on," Boyle replied.

"Thanks for the invitation to the game," Matt said.

"I haven't seen much of you in recent weeks." Boyle said. "If you have a few minutes, I'd like to share some thoughts with you. I don't want to talk about work at the game, and I'd like to give you some more of my rules for ministers. You heard the first four rules last fall."

"Go right ahead. I'd like to hear more of them."

Boyle reached into his middle desk drawer and pulled out a sheet of paper. "Here's my list. Let me quickly review the first four rules with you. Number one: make sure you know what's going on around you because knowledge is power and job security. Number two: try to give the church members what they want to hear. Third: know your biggest contributors and shower them with attention because you should know who's paying your salary. And fourth, which I hope you'll remember as you start to give more sermons around here: keep your sermons on a personal level and leave national and international issues out of them."

"Given your years of experience," Matt said, "I always appreciate hearing your thoughts. I think about the rules you gave me, although I'm not sure I agree with all of them. I agree that ministers should be careful about the words they choose when giving a sermon. On the other hand, I'm not sure pastors should know what their members give financially because it could result in favoritism. I'd be interested in hearing some more of your rules."

"Rule number five, Beringer, is don't work with a financial advisor in the congregation. In theory, a church member who's a financial advisor should want to help us ministers more than anyone. And I'm sure that most financial advisors are well intentioned. However, there was a situation during my Phoenix ministry where a member sold some investments to the senior pastor, who was my supervisor, as well as to a bunch of the members. This advisor pushed some real estate limited partnerships that went belly-up, and the senior pastor and the members who invested in them lost money. The senior pastor was forced to resign, and we lost quite a few members because of it. You know me. I like the stock market and the investment world, but I think it's risky to work with a financial advisor who's in the congregation. A minister's financial profile should be confidential, and you wouldn't want personal information like that to become known by the congregation because of an unintended mistake or an intentional leak."

"Sounds like great advice. Has anyone in the congregation tried to market financial services?"

"Ouch! I hoped you wouldn't ask that question. I must confess that I did invest in a real estate limited partnership with a member several years ago, and I lost my entire five-thousand-dollar investment. That hurt. I should have known better, especially after the

Phoenix disaster, but I obviously didn't. There were a handful of our members who lost money, too. The member was convicted of selling fraudulent investments, so I can speak about rule number five from personal experience."

"I'm sorry to hear that. That rule makes sense."

"Rule number six is don't share information about your financial activities. Church members are opinionated when it comes to pastors' salaries and lifestyles. I recently read *Mere Christianity* by C. S. Lewis, and it really turned me around about where my focus should be. One of the chapters discusses "the great sin," which is pride or self-conceit. Lewis says that pride leads to every other vice. Pride is about power, and it causes us to feel superior to others. I'm sure I told you at the beginning of our friendship that I drove a Lexus. I inherited it from my late aunt, and I was proud to have it because I couldn't afford to buy that kind of car. However, it was prideful of me to talk about my car, and I suspect that my self-promotion was not well received by the persons who had to listen to me."

"*Mere Christianity* is a book I need to read," Matt said. "I'm glad it made a positive impact on you. How many rules do you have for me?"

"I have ten on this list, and I could probably add a few more if I tried. Here's my third rule for today, and we'll leave it at that. Rule number seven is a minister should be a servant, not a king. After seminary, we start our work as ministers and think we have all the answers. We want to imprint our ideas and beliefs onto the church's operations and programs. However, I've learned through experience that effective and authentic ministry is a little different from that. We should instead be servants and help the congregation discover what its needs are. It's not about what we can do for the church, but rather, it's about how we can help the members discover what God wants for them."

"That's a good rule to follow," Matt said. "Sometimes our egos can get in the way of serving others. I know I've been guilty of that at various times."

"Exactly. We all have. I have at least three more rules to share with you, and I plan to do that before year-end." Boyle gave Matt a wink and a smile. "But that's enough for now. How's married life treating you?" Boyle asked.

"Sharing my life with Jancy has been wonderful. I've never been happier. I only wish my parents could be involved in our lives. Maybe they are."

"I know they'd like what they see," Boyle said.

"They'd also see that I've gained a few pounds since our wedding in June!" Matt laughed. "Besides being a wonderful partner, Jancy has many talents, including preparing delicious meals. She's really spoiling me. She's organized our apartment a little differently than when I lived there alone, so I sometimes have trouble finding things, which can be interesting. And we do the laundry more often than I did when I was single, which is a positive. All in all, I've really been blessed! Thanks for asking."

"Be careful about accumulating stuff," Boyle said. "It's amazing how much we collect through the years. And, in the end, who will want it? I've started to give away things that nobody will want after I pass away. Friendships are far more important than collecting stuff."

"Speaking of friendships, Jancy and I would like to have you over for dinner some evening. Is there a day that you would prefer over another?"

"Thanks for the invitation," Boyle said. "I'd enjoy that. I have theater tickets on some Friday and Saturday nights, so any other evening would be just fine."

"I'll discuss a date with Jancy, and I'll bring you several options tomorrow."

"Wonderful," Boyle said.

Matt checked his watch. "I need to prepare for my next meeting, so I should be on my way, but I have a question for you," Matt said. "I met an attorney the other day who is a member of the Esther Society. I've never heard of it. Do you know anything about it?"

"No," Boyle said. "Any relation to the Esther Scroll?"

"I don't think so," Matt said. "He said they're a global organization that wants to revive an interest in the Ten Commandments."

"Maybe it's a group of Orthodox Jews."

"Not exactly. He said the society is composed of both Christians and Jews. They're based in Jackson Hole, Wyoming. Their goal is to promote the Ten Commandments in a post-biblical world. That sounds fine to me, but why are they so secretive about it?"

"I wish I could help you," Boyle said, "but I don't know anything about them."

"You'd think we would have heard about them," Matt said.

"They sound well intentioned. How do they work to accomplish their goals, especially since we've never heard about them?"

"I don't have a clear picture of how they operate," Matt said, "but I want to learn more about the group, and I'll keep you posted."

"I'd like to hear more."

"Okay. I'm looking forward to going to the A's game with you," Matt said, rising from his chair.

"And I've enjoyed our conversation today, Matt. Thanks for the dinner invitation."

As Matt left Boyle's office, he remembered a crossword puzzle clue: "Diamond covering." The answer was "TARP." Given the warm weather, Matt was certain the groundskeepers at the Oakland Coliseum would not need to protect the baseball infield from rain on Saturday.

*I think that's the best conversation I've ever had with Pastor Boyle!* His supervisor had reached out in friendship and acted less defensive than in previous meetings.

# 9

THE NEXT DAY, PASTOR STALEY was standing at the counter, speaking to Mrs. Kirby, when Matt entered the church office to check his mailbox. It was a few minutes before eleven in the morning. Staley asked Matt if he had a few minutes to chat in his office. He didn't have an appointment until three o'clock, so he gladly accepted the invitation.

Matt followed the senior pastor down the hall to his large office overlooking the village of San Lucas and San Francisco Bay to the west. Staley settled into the chair behind his desk and motioned for Matt to sit in one of the two chairs facing him.

"I'm going to have a soda. Would you like to join me?" Staley asked, opening the small refrigerator beside his desk and retrieving a can for himself. He reached for a glass inside the credenza behind his desk.

"Sounds great," Matt replied. "Do you have a lemonade?"

"I think I do," Staley said, reaching into the refrigerator again for a can. After finding another glass in his credenza, he leaned across the desk and gave them both to Matt.

"It's a warm one today," Matt said, opening the can. "This will be refreshing."

"Now that you and I are trustees of the Staley Family Trust, I think we need to become experts on the contents of the scroll. Let's talk about the book of Esther. How does that sound?

"I'd enjoy that," Matt replied. "I've been thinking a lot about it since the article in the *East Bay Times*."

"Esther is not a very well-known book in the Bible," Staley said. "Have you ever read it?" Pastor Staley leaned back in his office chair and crossed his legs.

"I read it the day after I saw the article in the *East Bay Times*," Matt responded. "I'm embarrassed to say that I haven't spent as much time studying the historical books, from Joshua to Esther. How well do you know the book of Esther?"

"I knew almost nothing about Esther," Staley said. "Please don't share that piece of information with our members. They would probably be shocked. Right now, I'm reading as many articles as I can find."

"It's a powerful story, isn't it?" Matt said. "A young Jewish girl, Esther, becomes the wife of the emperor, Xerxes, and her royal status allows her to intervene and prevent the annihilation of the Jewish people. It's difficult not to see God's hand in protecting and saving his people through the events in the book, even though God is never mentioned."

"Yes," Staley said, "the book also explains the celebration of Purim—its origin, its tradition, and its observance. It helped establish a festival in Israel that may have been a Persian celebration adopted by the Jews during their exile. The author wanted to promote and continue the event in Jerusalem to commemorate the Esther story as Jews began to return to their homeland."

"It would be interesting to know how this scroll, with such an exotic story, found its way to your parents in New Jersey."

SECRET MOTIVES | 67

"I want to look into that, but I'm not sure where to begin," Staley said. "I suppose I could try contacting some of their friends, although most of them have died. Dad had a brother in Boston, but he passed away years ago. I'm not sure I'll ever find the answer."

"Wouldn't you agree there are some good reasons why Esther scrolls weren't found in the Qumran caves?" Matt asked.

"Yes," Staley said. "I'm sure it wasn't a favorite book of the Essene community because God is never mentioned. Also, the star of the story is a woman, who wouldn't have been a popular character among the all-male Essene community at Qumran."

"In addition," Matt said, "the Essenes may not have been interested in a story about a young Jewish woman marrying a Persian king. Finally, the focus on Persia and an opulent court setting—I counted ten feasts—which includes a harem and palace intrigues, would have turned off the Essenes. What surprises me is how critical biblical scholars have been toward the book, including Martin Luther, who said he wished it didn't exist."

"The fact that it was written in Persia, during the Exile, no doubt caused it to receive less attention than books with roots in Israel, like Isaiah and the Psalms. However, like you, I see God at work in this book, protecting and then intervening to save the Jews."

"The remarkable events in Esther," Matt said, "can only be explained by the invisible hand of God at work."

"At the heart of it," Staley said, "we have a young girl who was chosen from a national search to become the wife of the emperor. With God's help, she used her royal position, along with beauty, charm, and courage, with great effectiveness to intervene and prevent the destruction of her people. Mordecai tells her, 'And who knows but that you have come to royal position for such a time as this?' Clearly, she became a heroine through her vigorous defense of her people."

"I call it the 'Esther factor,'" Matt said, "where she undertakes an activity that pleases God. What Esther did and what we do when we pray, worship, study the Bible, and serve others are activities that please God. That should be our daily focus, to please God. At the same time, we see in Esther the hand of God, working out his plans and fulfilling his promises. It's an inspiring message."

"Changing the subject," Staley said, "I've been giving some thought to the woman you spotted at our house the other day, following the break-in. I decided to ask the neighbors if they know her."

"What did you learn?"

"We have several church members who live around us," Staley said. "I started with them. None of them knew of a household with a yellow Lab or a woman who walks one. I reported this information to the police, but I don't know what they can do with it. I'm wondering how she could be connected to our robbery."

"I wish I had a better memory of what she looked like. I don't think I could recognize her if I saw her again."

"Okay. I'll let you know if I learn anything more about her," Staley said. "Now, let's wrap up our discussion about Esther. It's interesting how often numbers like three, seven, ten, twelve, forty, and seventy appear in the narrative."

"I agree," Matt said. "I'm fascinated with the use of numbers in the Bible. The number seven is a Hebrew sacred number, and it often appears in the Old Testament. In Genesis, the seventh day completed the creation cycle and became the Sabbath. In the first chapter of Esther, the author used the number seven a total of three times. To me, sacred numbers describe God's presence in human history. There's also a political side to the story," Matt added. "Haman's decree against the Jews shows the anti-Semitic feeling in the ancient world. On one hand, the book of Joel reveals organized massacres of Jews in both Edom and Egypt. However, in this story, the Jews took matters into their own hands and forced non-Jews to become converts under fear of death. There was as much political intrigue in Esther's time as there is today."

"One of my favorite painters is Caravaggio," Staley said, "mainly because of the way he uses chiaroscuro. He contrasts light and dark to give the appearance of depth, and it creates a more dramatic effect. I liked the way the author used contrasts in the narrative to create a mood. The opening description of the king shows his authority and power, but later we see his passivity and weakness. In addition, there is the king's angry response to Queen Vashti when she fails to appear before him, compared to when Esther arrives unexpectedly, and he quickly offers her half of his kingdom! And another contrast involves one of the great ironies—the reversal of Haman's career. He was the prime minister, a favorite of King Xerxes, and persecuted the Jews, but he receives the punishment he plotted for them and is hanged on the gallows he had prepared for Mordecai!"

"The book is full of contrasts and reversals of fortune, that's for sure," Matt said.

"Well, we've had a lively conversation," Staley said. "I'm glad we had this talk. We've both been on a steep learning curve, and I'm pleased to know how interested you are in this book. It reinforces my belief that you were the right person to ask to become a trustee. Why don't we meet again in a couple of weeks and continue our conversation?"

"I look forward to it."

"There's another subject I'd like to discuss with you, if you have another minute."

"I do."

"Besides the Esther Scroll, I inherited about $250,000 from my parents' bank account in Paramus, and I'd like to invest the money rather than keep it in the bank. Rates aren't very high on certificates of deposit right now, and I've read that some stocks pay dividends around 3 or 4 percent. Before now, I've never had much extra money to invest in the stock market, but I'd like to become better acquainted with it. You do some stock investing, don't you?"

"Yes, I inherited twenty stocks from my parents, and I've added five names to our portfolio in the past two years. I spend a considerable amount of time each week following our portfolio, checking the stock market, and researching companies whose shares we might want to own at some point in the future.

"Could you help me figure out how to invest this money? Plus, there will be more money to invest when we sell my parents' house."

"I'd enjoy sharing some thoughts with you. When would you like to have a conversation about it?"

"How about a week from today, next Friday afternoon at two?"

"That will give me some time to think about a plan for you. I believe I can help you."

"Great! I'll visit your office around two."

Matt left their meeting feeling pleased that Staley had asked him for some investment assistance. He was confident he could help the Staleys develop a solid investment program.

# 10

IN HACIENDA'S MONTHLY *BELL TOWER* NEWSLETTER for August, the front-page article recognized Pastor and Mrs. Staley's ten years of service to the church. Under Pastor Staley's leadership, the membership had expanded from 750 members to over one thousand. The budget had nearly doubled. Domestic and global mission projects had grown, and the youth programs had flourished. Matt thought the article described a successful ministry.

If a vote were taken among the members, he guessed that the vast majority would be supportive of Staley's efforts. In Matt's short time at Hacienda, he had quickly formed an opinion about ministry. He observed that two skills are especially important for a minister's success: first, delivering meaningful sermons with a powerful biblical truth and, second, providing effective leadership to the Session, the elders who manage the church. Staley seemed to be performing well in both areas.

At the same time, Matt had heard a few members describe Staley as aloof. Matt thought he more closely fit the profile of a private person—friendly but at the same time reserved. Although Staley was fully engaged in his role as a minister, Matt spotted signs that his professional life at Hacienda may have been influenced by a painful incident in his previous ministry in La Jolla.

During Matt's internship the previous year, Staley had shared a deeply personal experience while giving him some advice about ministry. He described how he was forced out as the minister of the First Presbyterian Church of La Jolla because a woman he was counseling accused him of making a pass at her. Staley told Matt that he denied the accusation and thought the woman was seeking attention, especially from her husband, to revive their marriage. Matt sensed the event had traumatized Staley, who admitted that he wondered if his career as a minister was finished. After he left the La Jolla church, Staley took a year off and earned a degree in pastoral counseling and then applied for the position as senior pastor at Hacienda Presbyterian. Staley advised Matt to have a witness in the room when he was having a counseling session.

Matt believed the La Jolla episode had affected Staley's work habits, causing him to become more cautious. His life had been turned upside down by a lie—an untruth he couldn't prove because it was his word against another's. He noted that Staley carefully controlled his daily activities. When the senior pastor had counseling appointments, Mrs. Kirby was always present as a witness. His desk was clear and uncluttered, preventing others from seeing what he was doing. He kept his daily calendar in his middle desk drawer. At noon, he preferred going home to have lunch with his wife. And he left the church promptly at four forty-five, fifteen minutes before Mrs. Kirby, avoiding late afternoon drop-ins who would find him without his witness.

The *Bell Tower* article also described how Staley had streamlined the structure of the Session, the governing body at Hacienda, by reducing the number of committees from eleven to seven and the number of ruling elders from twenty to fourteen, which he had completed the previous year. Matt believed this project was consistent with Staley's interest in preventing the kind of conflict that hurt him in La Jolla. If Matt's assessment was correct, Staley was trying to promote harmony and reduce the chance of confrontations.

A smaller Session meant fewer reports and shorter meetings, another Staley priority, and it simplified the oversight of church operations. Fewer Session members allowed the Nominating Committee to be more selective in choosing future elders. Staley kept a tight rein on the meetings by assigning time limits to each agenda item, which encouraged the elders to make concise and relevant statements.

Matt knew Staley was not a big fan of evening meetings. Apart from the monthly Session meetings, Staley's schedule included very few nighttime commitments. He told Matt that, in his opinion, people become more disagreeable at the end of the day after hours spent at the office. Matt was certain that Staley's wish to avoid stressful evening meetings was a major reason for reorganizing the Session. He didn't want to strain the elders' patience or test their tempers.

After Matt finished reading the newsletter, he put it in his desk drawer. Tonight, he would see Staley's leadership style in action at the Session meeting. It was held on the third Tuesday, and Matt planned to return to Hacienda at seven o'clock.

Entering the Amigos Room, a little before seven, Matt found a chair in the second row. Pastor Staley was seated behind a table in front as the Session Moderator. Next to Staley sat the ruling elder, John Stallings, Clerk of Session. Stallings kept the minutes, along with maintaining the church's ledgers of membership, births, baptisms, deaths, and elders. Matt thought Stallings was perfect for his job. A retired CPA, he wore wire-rimmed glasses and was friendly but seldom smiled. He also sat at the scorer's table at the boys' high school basketball games, logging statistics for the officials and referees, as well as for the San Lucas coaches. Keeping records had become Stallings's retirement hobby. Matt noticed only one absentee, Pastor Boyle, which did not surprise Matt since Boyle had confessed a dislike for evening meetings. After working a full day, Boyle said that returning to church for another meeting was like having to work overtime, which he resented.

Carlo Barone, the church custodian, had set up a coffeemaker on a mobile cart against the wall, including two large plates of cookies. Matt walked over to the cart, filled a coffee cup, and wrapped two cookies in a napkin before returning to his chair.

The meeting focused primarily on committee reports. At the end of the reports, Daniel Kincaid, who had been a thorn in Matt's side during his brief time at Hacienda, raised his hand. "I heard that the chaperones found a couple cans of beer at the middle school dance two weeks ago, and I'd like Pastor Beringer to tell us what happened."

"Daniel," Staley said, frowning at the unexpected question, "that subject is not on our agenda, but I'll allocate five minutes to discuss it. Matt, can you provide a response to Daniel?"

Matt shifted in his chair, not expecting to speak at the Session meeting. "We found two half-full cans of beer," Matt said.

Kincaid interrupted, raising his voice. "They were found near the fountain outside the gym, and I'd like to know where they came from!"

"We don't know who brought them," Matt replied. "We emptied the cans and disposed of them. At intermission, we told the kids that beer is not allowed on church property. I said that violating the rules could result in the cancellation of future dances. After that, the dance continued without any problems."

"Well, I can't believe that the chaperones didn't see the kids arrive with the beer," Kincaid said. "Did you have enough supervision?"

"We had two other couples," Matt said, "in addition to Jancy and me. About one hundred kids attended the dance. I think we had adequate supervision."

"I don't know why dances have to be part of our Christian education program," Kincaid interjected, standing up. "What do dances have to do with the Bible, anyway?" he asked, turning to face Matt. Kincaid's fists were clenched.

"I want the kids to think of Hacienda as their home away from home," Matt said. "Christian education involves more than Bible study, as important as that is. We want to support activities for the kids that involve positive interactions with their peers. The middle school principal appreciates our help in hosting two summer dances when the kids aren't in school. The school plans to host three dances during the school year. I shared this plan with the members of the Christian Education Committee, and they support our sponsorship."

"It seems to me that we're encouraging bad habits," Kincaid said, "like drinking beer in middle school."

"I don't think that finding a couple of half-empty beer cans is a very serious problem," another elder added. "Let's move onto the next agenda item."

"Now wait a minute," Kincaid shouted. "I haven't heard how they got there."

"As I said," Matt replied, "we couldn't determine who brought the beer. The two cans could have been left by the landscape crew that afternoon. Right now, we have more serious addiction issues in our middle schools across the nation. I read a recent study that said nearly one in twelve eighth grade students admitted to drinking alcohol on a monthly basis. Marijuana has now surpassed traditional cigarettes in middle school smoking rates. Five percent of eighth graders say they've used inhalants, like gasoline and paint thinner. Our kids know we don't endorse alcohol or drug consumption, so I think we can put the two cans of beer behind us."

Pastor Staley cleared his throat. "Daniel, I appreciate your concerns. There are several elements to our Christian faith.

Studying the Bible is one of them. Number two is worship; number three is prayer; and number four is community. I see these middle school dances as part of what we do to strengthen our church community."

"I disagree," Kincaid said, putting his hands on his hips. "I think the dances are totally unnecessary. The kids need to learn what's in the Bible. The bottom line is that I'm unhappy with Beringer's middle school leadership, and I think he needs to be replaced. I think I could do a better job!"

Despite Staley's efforts to restructure the Session to reduce potential conflicts, the meeting had taken an ominous turn.

"I'm sorry you feel that way," Staley said. "I know you were also critical of the two previous middle school leaders. Matt has my endorsement, as well as the full support of the Education Committee. He's just starting his work as a full-time staff member, Daniel, so I hope you'll give him some slack before drawing conclusions."

"I'm also unhappy that you chose Beringer to be a trustee of your family trust," Kincaid said. "I've grown up in this church, have been a member for forty years, and have been an elder for almost three years. Matt's been here for just one year, and you chose him to oversee the Esther Scroll. Why didn't you consider me?"

"I think we're wandering way off course," another elder said. "The Esther Scroll is Pastor Staley's inheritance and has nothing to do with this evening's agenda. Let's move on to the next item."

"Thanks, Steve," Pastor Staley said. "I don't want to avoid your question, Daniel, but this isn't the time or place to discuss your question in depth. Briefly, I asked Matt to become a trustee because he's much younger than Joan and I are, and we hope he'll be around to manage our trust after we retire and have passed away. He's a colleague of mine with a similar educational background and professional career, and Joan and I thought he would be a very good choice."

"Pastor Staley, will you tell us about your request for more support for Mrs. Kirby?" another elder asked. "That's the next agenda topic."

Daniel Kincaid sat down with a scowl on his face and crossed his arms. "You haven't heard the last of my complaints," he muttered.

Staley looked at some papers on the table to find his notes. "As our membership has grown over the past ten years, the Administration Committee has periodically considered hiring an additional office employee to assist Mrs. Kirby. Due to my recent inheritance, I've seen her workload grow. We've had a large increase in phone calls and letters, in addition to more visitors coming to the office. I've spoken to the Administration Committee, and they're receptive to the idea of hiring another staff member as a full-time receptionist. I've agreed to pay half of the new employee's salary. They think they can find the remaining funds without disrupting the church budget."

"Sounds like a great idea to me," said Mike Jensen, head of Finance. "It's generous of Pastor Staley to help with the cost of a new employee. Right now, our revenues are ahead of our budget, so I think we can afford it."

Matt liked Mike Jensen, an owner of an insurance agency in San Francisco. Mike and Jean Jensen had asked Jancy and him to join them on a picnic in Napa Valley during Matt's internship.

"I'm going to protest a little if it comes out of our budget," responded Steve Canfield, head of the Mission Committee and a pediatrician in Oakland. "I've been around long enough to know the Mission budget is often the first to be cut when a new project arises."

"I don't think you have to worry about it, Steve," Jensen replied. "We won't have to cut anyone's budget."

"That brings me to another subject, Steve," Staley said, "and it's not on the agenda. I'd like to plant a seed with you and your committee. I'd like to establish a foundation here at Hacienda to raise funds to supplement and expand our Mission budget. A foundation would allow us to encourage, receive, and manage gifts and donations in perpetuity. Investment income generated by the foundation would be added to our local and global mission budgets to expand those programs. Members and San Lucas citizens could remember our foundation in their wills to make a long-term commitment to Hacienda and to mission work."

"I like your idea," Steve said. "I'll take it to the committee, and we'll consider it."

"Getting back to Mrs. Kirby," Staley said, "do you have a motion for us to consider, David?"

"Yes, I do," said David Marshall, chair of the Administration Committee. "I move that we hire a full-time receptionist with the salary and benefits to be determined by our committee before the interviewing process begins, and with the expenses to be shared evenly between the church and Pastor Staley."

"I second the motion," Jensen said.

Staley repeated the motion and called for a vote, which passed unanimously. "Thanks for your good work this evening," he said. "Let's close our meeting with a word of prayer."

The meeting had run a few minutes late, and Matt could see that Staley was eager to leave.

Before going home, Matt decided to visit Carlo Barone, whose office was next to the gym on the other side of the administration building. Seeing across the courtyard that Carlo's door was open and his light was on, Matt turned right from the Amigos Room and walked down the hall toward Staley's office, then turned left, and headed toward the gym. Turning left again, he arrived at Carlo's office and saw him seated at his desk. "Carlo, do you have a few minutes?"

"Sure. Come on in, Matt. I haven't seen you in a while. What church problems have you been solving lately?"

"We had a Session meeting tonight, as you know." Matt settled into a chair in front of Carlo's desk. "Thanks for setting up a coffee-maker and providing the cookies. They added a lot to the meeting."

"Happy to do it. The meeting was on my calendar."

"Pastor Boyle was the only one absent tonight. He told me he doesn't like evening meetings."

"I've noticed that Charlie's been a little moody recently," Carlo said.

"He surprised me recently by apologizing for bragging to me last year that he drove a Lexus. He said he'd read a book that made him realize he was wrong."

"Charlie's fifty-eight or thereabouts, and I'm guessing he's at that stage where he's evaluating his life. He's probably thinking about retirement and wonders if he can stay here until that time or whether he'll need to make another move. I'll bet he'd like to retire here at Hacienda."

"Yeah," Matt said. "He's had quite a few jobs over the past twenty years, prior to Hacienda, so I'm sure he's tired of moving."

"I think Charlie's string of disappointments has taken its toll: his divorce after eight or nine years of an unhappy marriage, being estranged from his daughter, and his numerous short-lived ministries. Charlie has finally achieved some stability in his life here at Hacienda, and I think he's afraid of losing it. He hasn't made many close friends here in the past eight years, partly because the failures in his important relationships have affected his ability to trust other people."

"Are you sure you're not a psychoanalyst on your days off?"

"As you know, Charlie and I go back many years here in Oakland. He grew up in a poor family, and that has influenced his outlook on life. He felt insecure as a youth, and he's been chasing security all his life. However, security and stability have been elusive goals for him. He didn't like being poor, and material comforts are important to him. You might say he guards them," Carlo said, smiling."

"Could he be mellowing?"

"I think so. Now that Pastor Staley has become a millionaire by inheriting the Esther Scroll, Charlie could be worried that Staley's going to retire, which would threaten his job security. A new pastor might want to bring in his own staff."

"Carlo, you've helped me better understand Charlie's current situation. I can see why he may be at that stage where he's reassessing things."

"Charlie is lonely. Beginning and end of story. Maybe you and he should have dinner before the Session meetings. Developing a friendship with Charlie might help him change his attitude toward the Session. Dealing with the church's future at the meetings probably makes Charlie very uncomfortable because of his history of past disappointments. You might give him the support he needs to face the future here."

"That's a good idea. I hate to miss dinners with Jancy, but I think she'd understand how a dinner once a month with Pastor Boyle could help him. Jancy and I recently talked about inviting him to dinner. Thanks, Carlo. I learn a lot about this place whenever I speak with you."

"I look forward to our next conversation!"

"I have one more question. What do you know about Daniel Kincaid?"

Carlo frowned. "I think Kincaid is a very troubled man."

"How so?"

"I think he feels short-changed in life, and he's very angry about it. As is often the case, he has no one to blame but himself. He grew up in a very successful San Lucas family. His father accumulated numerous commercial real estate properties, which are very valuable, and now Daniel manages them. His older brother is a surgeon, and his younger sister owns a very successful executive search firm in San Francisco that does a lot of work with Silicon Valley companies. She's supposed to be very dynamic and energetic. Daniel appears to be the underachiever in the family."

"Is he married?"

"Twice divorced. No kids."

"He was confrontational toward me last year at a party I attended at the Canfields' condo in San Francisco. He criticized me tonight at the Session meeting and even questioned why Pastor Staley chose me to be a trustee of the Staley Family Trust. He said he was more qualified to be the trustee."

"I'd be careful around that guy. He had troubles with the San Lucas police when he was a teenager. He was playing with matches in a vacant lot near his home when he was thirteen or fourteen and started a fire. His dad tried to get the fire department to forget about it, but they cited Daniel for mischief and starting the fire. When he was a little older, around fifteen or sixteen and before he had his driver's license, the San Lucas Police caught him trying to steal a car. He said he wanted to take it for a joy ride, but he could have been in an accident and hurt people."

"I'm sorry to hear all that."

"I don't know why Pastor Staley wanted him on the Session," Carlo said. "Maybe it was an attempt to help the guy."

"He seems to have a very bad temper," Matt said.

"I'd stay away from him, Matt," Carlo said. "He's a loose cannon, and you don't want to be around him when he explodes."

"I'll follow your advice."

"Plus, Kincaid has an alcohol problem. He's received numerous DUI tickets from the San Lucas Police. They're well acquainted with him."

"On that note, I think I'll be on my way, Carlo," Matt. "Thanks again for your wise counsel."

Matt returned to the church office the way he came, tracing the partial outline of the courtyard. After checking his mailbox, he walked through the double doors and into the warm evening as the last rays of twilight disappeared in the west. Seeing Jancy at home in fifteen minutes would lift his spirits. He decided to stop at the neighborhood supermarket and buy her a bouquet of flowers.

———◆———

LATER, WHEN MATT AND JANCY went to bed, he said to her, "One of the Session members criticized my leadership of the youth program."

"Who was that?"

"Daniel Kincaid. He's in his third and final year as an elder on the Session. Pastor Staley said that Kincaid hasn't been a positive contributor to the Session. In fact, he's been increasingly critical of the church over the past three years, especially about the youth programs. Tonight, he said he could do a better job of leading the youth ministry than I am. I can't believe he's serious about wanting that responsibility."

"I remember Kincaid, but he didn't have any kids in the children's program, so I never became acquainted with him."

"I stopped by Carlo's office after the meeting, and he filled me in on Kincaid's rather checkered past."

"He sounds like someone to avoid."

"I agree. Kincaid even asked Staley why he chose me to become a trustee of the Staley Family Trust. He said he thought he was more qualified and deserving!"

"Is he mentally stable?" Jancy asked. "Could he be dangerous?"

"Possibly. He's been critical of previous interns, as well."

"I'm sorry to hear about this. Please be careful around him," Jancy said. "And now, I have to go check on the clothes dryer. It's almost finished its cycle. Then, let's go to sleep."

While Jancy was gone, Matt wondered if it might have been Daniel Kincaid who was driving the car that rear-ended him on the Nimitz Freeway. *He has a driving record to prove that he's a menace behind the wheel, and by killing me, he might think he could succeed me as trustee of the Staley Family Trust.*

# 11

Mrs. Kirby called Matt to tell him that the visitor from Switzerland was a few minutes early for his appointment. Matt left his office and descended the stairs to welcome the man from Geneva, who had requested an eleven o'clock meeting with Pastor Staley to discuss the Esther Scroll. Staley was called on short notice to conduct a funeral service and wasn't available to meet with Bertrand Delacroix and had asked Matt to speak with him in his place.

When Matt entered the office, Delacroix was sitting in one of two upholstered chairs, separated by a table, sipping a cup of coffee. He had been reading the *East Bay Times*. As Matt approached Delacroix, he put the newspaper aside, stood up, and offered his hand. His slender fingers and palm matched his lean build. Although his grip was firm, Delacroix's skin was soft, suggesting to Matt that he didn't work with his hands. The visitor stood about five six and wore gray slacks and a blue blazer, with an off-white dress shirt, open at the collar.

"Greetings, Mr. Delacroix," Matt said. "I'm Matt Beringer, an associate of Pastor Staley. Unfortunately, he isn't available to meet with you due to a death in our congregation. He was asked to preside over the funeral this morning. For now, he suggested I speak with you, but if your schedule permits, he'd like to plan another meeting with you. Do you have time for a conversation?"

"Yes, certainly," Delacroix said. "I'm sorry to hear Reverend Staley has been called away, but he's where he should be, providing comfort to those who have suffered a loss."

"Let's go to Pastor Staley's office," Matt said, "and discuss why you've come all this way." He held the door open and gestured down the hall toward the senior pastor's office. Delacroix brought his cup of coffee and briefcase, and the two walked in silence in the corridor. Reaching the office door, Matt opened it for his guest. "How was your trip?"

"Very uneventful," he said, "which is the way I like to travel."

Following his guest into Pastor Staley's office, Matt motioned for Delacroix to take a chair in front of the minister's large desk. Matt settled into Pastor Staley's leather chair, while the diminutive figure in front of him took a seat in the first of two chairs facing the desk. Delacroix placed his coffee cup on the desk and his briefcase on the adjacent chair. Matt noticed that he rubbed his right jaw.

Delacroix had a flawless, fair complexion, slightly tanned, and a full head of brown hair, graying at the temples. Matt gauged a man's interest in his own apparel by the quality of his belt and shoes, and Delacroix wore the finest of both. His belt was made of alligator skin, possibly from Italy. He wore expensive, dark-brown leather shoes with tassels. There were no wrinkles at the elbows of his jacket, indicating it had been recently pressed, further signaling to Matt that his guest paid attention to details or liked to impress; Matt had yet to decide. Once again, Delacroix rubbed his chin and the sides of his face.

"I recently became a trustee of the Staley Family Trust that owns the scroll, so I'll be very involved with it going forward," Matt said.

"Thank you for speaking with me today, Reverend Beringer," Delacroix said. "I hope we can reschedule another meeting when I can meet with both of you."

"I know Pastor Staley would like that. Can I refill your cup of coffee?" Matt asked.

"No, thank you," he replied. "I had a late breakfast at a restaurant in Jack London Square, so this cup will be enough."

"You're a long way from home," Matt said.

"I have an ownership interest in a Napa Valley winery, so I try to fly into San Francisco at least once a year, usually during the grape harvest."

"This is a wonderful time to visit the Bay Area. How long will you be here?" Matt asked.

"At least two months," he replied. "I arrived yesterday and will spend a few days in San Francisco before traveling north to the wine country."

"August is a very busy time for the wineries," Matt said.

Delacroix leaned forward and placed his business card on the desk.

Matt reached for it and glanced at the printing on one side. On the other side was the colorful coat of arms of the Delacroix family.

"As I mentioned in my letter, I read an article in a Swiss newspaper about the first-ever appearance of the Esther Scroll. Since I planned to visit Napa Valley, I had hoped to meet with Reverend Staley and learn a little more about his inheritance. On the airplane, I read several articles about the Dead Sea Scrolls. I even brought a book about the scrolls I plan to read. Although I doubt Reverend Staley has made any decisions about what he wants to do with the scroll, I want to be one of the first in line to express an interest in acquiring it."

"What attracts you to the scroll?"

"I'm a collector and investor. My mother took me to see the *Mona Lisa* in the Louvre when I was twelve, and I decided then and there that I wanted to collect art involving beautiful women."

"I wouldn't describe the Esther Scroll as a traditional piece of art," Matt replied.

"I agree, but Esther is a feminine name," he said, "and the article I read piqued my interest in the scroll. My collecting interests and activities are quite broad. I recently read the book of Esther in the Old Testament for the first time and quite enjoyed it. Esther was a heroic young woman."

"I agree with you. Since all this has happened, I've also been reading articles about the book of Esther." Matt paused before continuing. "Did you grow up in Geneva?"

"I was born and educated in Paris," he replied, "and I moved to Geneva twenty-five years ago for business reasons. I have homes in Paris and Florence, as well as Geneva. I own an accounting firm, based in Geneva, and have people who manage it, allowing me to pursue my hobbies. I also own an interest in several wineries, including the one I mentioned in Napa Valley. A certain amount of travel is part of my lifestyle these days. Do you know if Reverend Staley is interested in selling the scroll?"

"I can't say," Matt said, "We've had it authenticated by Dead Sea Scroll experts, and now we're in the process of having it appraised. He may want to sell it in the future, but we haven't crossed that bridge yet."

"As I mentioned, I'm here today to let you know I'm very interested in acquiring it," Delacroix said. "I'd like you to get to know me, and I'd like to become better acquainted with Reverend Staley and you."

"Pastor Staley is planning to work for a few more years, but when he retires, he may want to sell the scroll to increase his financial flexibility. I know he has philanthropic interests he'd like to pursue in the future. However, it could be several years before any decisions are made about what to do with the scroll."

"Maybe I could interest him in taking an earlier retirement," Delacroix said with a smile.

"I will tell him about your interest in the scroll. While he enjoys the ministry, I can't predict how he might respond to a financial offer for it. Can you tell me a little about your art collection?" Matt asked.

"Yes. A major part of my collection includes paintings of ballerinas by Degas. I also own a couple of Renoirs."

"Do you focus on the Impressionists?"

"Yes, I'm especially fond of them. I also own some lithographs of female dancers by Lautrec and numerous sculptures of women, as well as first-edition books about famous women."

"You certainly have followed through on your decision to collect art revolving around women."

"My family was an early investor in the Nestlé company, so I'm fortunate to have more than adequate annual income. However, I'm a little like Toulouse-Lautrec, who came from a wealthy family and didn't have to work. He wanted to be successful on his own, apart from his family's resources, and so did I."

Both men looked at each other for a moment, Matt considering whether Delacroix was a possible buyer for the scroll, although something about him and his interests gave Matt pause. Was the visitor legit, given the very narrow focus of his collection? And Delacroix seemed bothered by something Matt couldn't quite identify. His gestures were fidgety, and he kept touching his face.

Delacroix continued. "I have a long-standing fondness for members of the opposite sex, going back to the day I saw the *Mona Lisa*. Unfortunately, I've been married three times, and recently divorced, so I don't seem able to hold onto women unless they're inanimate objects I own. When I heard about the Esther Scroll being inherited by Reverend Staley, I was drawn to it because of its name and decided to learn more about the Dead Sea Scrolls. Studying the history of the scrolls and the Qumran community has been interesting. As I mentioned, I acquire art and historical items if they involve attractive women—and have some investment merit to them."

"Are you thinking of making an offer for the scroll?" Matt asked.

"Yes, I'm prepared to make an offer. And I won't quibble about the price you set. From my reading, I expect to pay over a million dollars."

At that point, Delacroix reached for his face, as he had before, but this time with both hands at his chin, he pulled upward, removing a face mask. Then he put it on his lap.

Matt's jaw dropped. His body tensed, and his breath caught in his throat. Thrown completely off guard, Matt was at a loss for words. A wave of anxiety swept over him. For a moment, he wondered if he was facing an impostor and if he might be in danger. He stared at the visitor.

"I'm sorry to have startled you," Delacroix said. "I should have explained my situation. I sometimes wear this thing in foreign countries, and today it was making my face itch. I've felt uncomfortable ever since I arrived this morning. Because of my wealth, I deal with some security issues, and I've developed a set of disguises." He placed the mask on top of his briefcase in the chair next to him.

Matt was unable to hide his discomfort. Delacroix's sudden action had unsettled him, and he was unnerved that he hadn't been given a warning. The visitor from Geneva wasn't nearly as handsome as his artificial mask. His skin wasn't as smooth or tanned, and his other features didn't match those of the disguise. "You surprised me. I never expected it," Matt confessed.

"I have to worry about being kidnapped," Delacroix said, taking out a handkerchief and wiping his brow. "And I don't want to get involved in ransom payments."

"Do you think you're a target?"

"I know I am. I associate with a group of global collectors who attend auctions, and we're followed by some nefarious characters. We're also a competitive group, with rivalries among our members, and each of us is used to getting his way. Not everyone can win, so sometimes egos are hurt when someone is outbid for an item. I try to keep a very low profile."

"Never a dull moment, it appears."

"You're quite right." Delacroix said, putting his mask inside his briefcase. "I think I've taken enough of your time today. It was good of you to see me today," he said, rising slowly from his chair. "This has been a helpful first meeting. I understand Pastor Staley may not know what he wants to do with the scroll, but I want to express my interest in acquiring it. I think there's time for me to schedule another meeting with Pastor Staley while I'm in the Bay Area. In fact, I'd like to have a couple more meetings with you both before I leave for Geneva at the end of October. You can always reach me on my cell phone. My goal is to return to Geneva with the Esther Scroll."

"This has been an interesting meeting," Matt said, standing up from his chair. His legs felt light as air and unsteady. "I'll give you a call after I speak with Reverend Staley. And I'll alert him about your disguise," Matt said with a slight grin.

Both men walked from Staley's office and started down the corridor.

"Can I call a cab for you?" Matt offered.

"No, thanks. I have a car waiting outside. I look forward to speaking with you again soon."

Matt walked with Delacroix to the building exit, held the door open for him, and wished him a good day. He watched the visitor saunter toward his waiting limousine and the car pull slowly out of the church parking lot.

When Matt returned to his office, he sank into his desk chair. Exhausted, he slumped his head on his arms that rested on the desk. *What have I gotten myself into by agreeing to be a trustee of the Staley Family Trust? Delacroix is a piece of work! Who is this collector from Geneva who took off his face?*

Matt had gathered some useful information about the man. One, he presented himself as a formidable collector of items related to women, especially attractive women. Two, money seemed to be no object in his quest for what he fancied. And three, Delacroix described himself as a tenacious competitor, used to getting what he wanted.

*To what lengths will he go to acquire the Esther Scroll?*

# 12

I NTERESTED IN LEARNING MORE about the Esther Society, Matt called George Wall a few days after their meeting and arranged to have lunch with him the following week. They met at a restaurant in Oakland's Jack London Square on a Friday in late August. After they were seated and served glasses of water, they reviewed their menus and gave their selections to the waiter.

"Have you eaten at this restaurant before?" Wall asked.

"No," Matt responded. "I rarely have lunch in Oakland, but I've heard good things about it."

"I've never had a bad meal here," Wall said, "so I hope you like what you ordered."

"Halibut is a favorite," Matt said. "I really enjoy seafood dishes."

"As I mentioned to you, my wife is interested in moving to San Lucas," Wall said. "She's heard positive things about the school district. We have a twelve-year-old daughter and a nine-year-old son. I've been commuting to Oakland from Milpitas for the past five years. You mentioned you live in San Leandro. How do you like working in San Lucas?"

"It has a small-town atmosphere," Matt said, "and I like the relaxed pace of life. I've enjoyed getting acquainted with some of the business owners in the village. There are a good number of sports programs for young people, and your kids might enjoy attending the activities at Hacienda Presbyterian. The school district has a good reputation. I think you'd like San Lucas."

"How did you find your way to Hacienda Presbyterian?"

"I attended Calvin Seminary in San Francisco and was interested in an internship opportunity at the church because it involved organizing a middle school basketball program. The sport is a favorite of mine. I played basketball in school, including my years at Princeton, and I'm still involved in a men's league at the Hayward Y."

"Given your height, I wondered if you played basketball," Wall said. "I'm glad to hear your positive comments about San Lucas."

"It has a lot going for it. It's a well-designed community in a beautiful setting. It's quiet and safe, and the residents appear to be successful and productive. People seem happy to be living there."

"Music to my ears," Wall said.

"At the same time," Matt said, "I've noticed some social pressures that seem exaggerated because San Lucas is so affluent. For example, kids can be defined by whether they live in upper or lower San Lucas, which seems crazy to me."

"That kind of stuff isn't new to me. I experienced it in Southern California, where I grew up," Wall said. "Tell me about your work at Hacienda."

"After the internship and seminary graduation in May, I was invited to join the staff as an assistant minister, primarily focusing on the middle school and high school programs," Matt said. "I'm in the process of formulating the program, and I'd like the kids to think of Hacienda as their second home. I want them to acquire an understanding of some subjects that will help guide them throughout their lives. By that I mean concepts they might not discuss very much at home, such as grace, gratitude, and forgiveness. Plus, I want them to develop a friendship with Jesus and his teachings, like the parables. If I can provide positive experiences for them, my wish is they'll want to belong to a church community for the rest of their lives."

"I like what I'm hearing," Wall responded. "Living in San Lucas would cut my commuting distance in half. That also appeals to me."

"I hope you can make that happen," Matt said.

"If my wife and I go house-hunting in San Lucas some afternoon, I'll call ahead, and maybe you could give us a tour of Hacienda Presbyterian."

"I'd enjoy doing that," Matt said. "Because of our conversation in Mr. Ferguson's office, I'm interested in hearing more about how the Esther Society promotes the Ten Commandments. I'd like to figure out a way to incorporate them into our youth programs at Hacienda. As people try to push the church out of the town square in our country, I agree with you that the Ten Commandments aren't receiving the attention they deserve."

"That's the way I feel," Wall said. "The American church continues to lose members, and our Judeo-Christian values are being replaced by alternative agendas. In fact, Christians and Jews are under attack around the world."

"I haven't had time to think about how to include the Ten Commandments in our educational format, but I hope you can give me a few ideas."

"I think the Fifth Commandment is a theme you could use effectively. It says, 'Honor your father and your mother, so that you may live long in the land the Lord your God is giving you.' It should be a central commandment for our youth to know and follow. Maybe you could plan some events for both your kids and their parents, such as having a speaker of faith who would stress the importance of family. Perhaps well-known male and female athletes could talk about how their families helped them succeed in sports. Maybe a professor from UC Berkeley could give a presentation on an important historical figure like Benjamin Franklin or Abigail Adams. Family life in Colonial times was not easy, but strong families like theirs allowed them to accomplish great things. The overall focus in your program could be on the family, which is the building block of civilization and the way our values are passed along from one generation to the next."

"I like your idea of having speakers who would discuss the family as a way to educate the kids about the Fifth Commandment," Matt said.

"In Jim Ferguson's office last week, I also mentioned the Fourth Commandment, 'Remember the Sabbath day and keep it holy.' Society would be healthier if we did a better job of spending one day each week giving thanks for our blessings, rather than chasing the almighty dollar seven days a week. This commandment also asks for the proper treatment of animals, and that could lead into a discussion of how we treat our animals, including our pets. With so many families having pets, that subject should resonate with your kids, as well as their parents. As I said last week, the Fourth and Fifth Commandments are unique among the Ten Commandments because they require positive action. The other commandments tell us what to avoid."

"It sounds like the Fourth and Fifth Commandments would work well together in a one-year curriculum," Matt said.

"I agree," Wall said.

"You've given me some great ideas for our youth programs. Thank you. I appreciate the chance to speak with you."

"You're welcome. Anytime. If you plan to discuss the Fourth or Fifth Commandments with any of your youth groups, I would enjoy attending one of your sessions. I'd like to report to our organization about how you used them in your educational program."

"I'll keep you posted," Matt said. "I have just one more question. Why does your society keep such a low profile?"

Wall grinned. "We're trying to use moderation rather than megaphones to make our case. We want to be humble in all we do."

"Can you send me some printed information about your group?" Matt asked.

"I will," Wall responded.

Matt and Wall continued their conversation, switching to sports and movies, before they concluded their lunch together. Wall insisted on paying, and Matt said he'd cover their next lunch together. He headed to his car, needing to return to Hacienda for his two o'clock discussion about investments with Pastor Staley.

———•———

MATT SUFFERED A CRUSHING LOSS five years before when his parents were killed unexpectedly in an auto accident during his senior year at Princeton. The protective envelope they provided had been torn away and, as an only child, he felt vulnerable and alone. Without their love and support, his life became complicated and opaque. The boundaries of the world in which he operated expanded instantly. His perspective shifted quickly from the familiar, such as basketball and his senior thesis, to the unfamiliar, such as his entire financial future. He suddenly became responsible for everything, especially matters dealing with dollars and cents. After graduation, he faced some large monetary decisions. Returning to Seattle, he had to sort and sell his parents' possessions that he didn't need and rent a self-storage facility to hold the items he wanted to save. He elected to simplify his life by selling his parents' home, rather than renting it as an absentee landlord. Still, he was overwhelmed by the responsibilities of managing the modest investment portfolio he inherited, along with the proceeds from the sale of the house.

Once the sale closed, he needed to find a home for those dollars. Investing the money became a priority. He subscribed to a variety of investment resources, such as the *Wall Street Journal, Barron's,* and *Value Line Investment Survey,* and reading those publications kept him busy. Matt leaned on his parents' financial advisor in Seattle for some guidance but decided to become an investment expert, rather than rely on someone else's financial counsel. After five years of continual study, Matt felt as if he had a good grasp of the world of stocks, bonds, and mutual funds.

———•———

RELAXING IN HIS OFFICE a few minutes before two, after his lunch with Wall, Matt heard a knock on his office door. "Come in!"

Pastor Staley entered Matt's office and looked around the room, as if he were seeing its contents for the first time.

"Have a seat," Matt said, as Staley stood in the middle of the room.

"I think I'll sit down in this sofa over here," Staley said, "and I can set my notebook next to me."

"Sure. Make yourself comfortable."

"I'm embarrassed to say that I think this is the first time I've visited your office since you started working with us."

"I'm sorry I can't offer you a beverage from a refrigerator near my desk, as you have in your office, but that's a goal of mine," Matt said.

"I should have brought a couple of cans with me. I've been impressed by how long and hard you work around here. Youth leaders like you have very stressful jobs. I was a youth minister once, and I've never worked so hard in my life! There were never enough hours in the day! You may find your work becomes easier as your ministry progresses."

"*Your* work doesn't appear easy to me, Pastor Staley," Matt said, "but a declining level of stress over time would be a positive."

"How do you want to start our investment conversation today?" Staley asked.

"Let's discuss how we might structure an investment program for the money you inherited. If you plan to invest for five years or longer, I think a conservative portfolio of thirty to thirty-five individual stocks is the way to go. The stock market has been high because it has benefited from interest rates that have been in a long-term downtrend since 1981, and there isn't much competition for stocks right now among low-yielding bonds and bank certificates of deposit. Therefore, I think you should proceed slowly to invest in the stock market. There are almost always attractive opportunities available, and you might consider investing two-thirds of the $250,000 over the next one to two years."

"That sounds reasonable to me. What about stock mutual funds?"

"I believe there are a limited number of great stock mutual fund managers, and if their funds do well, the assets under management can grow to enormous sizes. Mutual fund investors often want to buy last year's best performing funds. However, chasing a top-performing fund can backfire. A fund portfolio may not continue to be as attractive as it was before its great year because it may be overvalued. In addition, the profile of a fund today with five or ten billion dollars under management changes dramatically if it grows to fifty billion dollars over several years, which can make it more difficult to manage. As a larger fund, it will need to own many more stocks, as well as the stocks of larger companies, in order to maintain sufficient diversity. On the other hand, if a fund's performance declines, investors will withdraw their money, and it's an additional challenge for a fund manager to perform well when selling stocks daily to meet share redemptions.

"Some managers," Matt continued, "who are under pressure to perform may try to trade their way to success, rather than focus on long-term investing. The turnover rate in most stock funds is around 100 percent annually, meaning that the typical fund manager holds his or her average stock for one year, which isn't investing to me. I call that trading, rather than investing. Trading stocks will also result in additional transaction expenses that subtract from the performance of a fund. Finally, fund managers can leave or retire, and sometimes the fund with a great past performance is no longer being managed by the person who established that record."

"I've never considered that a fund's performance may have resulted from the work of a previous fund manager," Staley said. "That would be an important subject to investigate."

"My feeling is there are too many variables in stock mutual fund investing that are beyond an investor's control. By comparison, I think that selecting a basket of thirty to thirty-five stocks that pay and will increase their dividends will be less expensive, generate the income and returns you seek, and give you greater control over your investment program. If you select the stocks, you know what you own, and your account size is not influenced by other investors adding or subtracting their money to it, as occurs with a mutual fund. Also, you can control your expenses and tax consequences by limiting your stock sales, and you don't have to worry about a fund manager leaving or retiring."

"What do I need to know as we start to think about building a stock portfolio?"

"In the short time I've been studying investments, I'm amazed that our capitalist economic system offers such a wide range of investment opportunities. Compared to other countries, we have the most investment options. Almost everything we read about can be connected to a potential investment—real estate, natural resources, recreation, entertainment, and information technology are just a few areas."

"I'm starting a little late in life, but I've had a growing interest in learning about the investment markets," Staley said. "Please continue."

"I'd like to share three very different truths that I've discovered that show how interesting the investment world can be. I think you will find your study of Wall Street markets challenging and engaging. First, there's a historical component to investing. You need to be aware of the behavior of interest rates over time. For example, stocks would be less attractive today if investors could earn 10 percent on certificates of deposit with no risk at their local bank. Now, however, with interest rates at low levels, stocks have become very popular because fixed-income alternatives aren't very competitive. That scenario is changing. Let's discuss interest-rate cycles."

"I've never even considered interest-rate cycles," Staley said.

"There have only been seven US interest-rate cycles, going back to 1798, and they last about thirty years but have varied from twenty-two to now thirty-nine years! A cycle is defined as a trend over time, reflected in a chart, that goes from a trough to a peak or a peak to a trough. Interest rates declined from 1798 to 1825, a twenty-seven-year period. They rose for thirty-six years from 1825 to 1861. The next cycle ran from a high in 1861 to a low in 1898, which was thirty-seven years. That cycle was followed by rising interest rates from 1898 to 1920, representing twenty-two years. The next cycle started in 1920 and lasted to 1946 for twenty-six years, followed by another cycle, from 1946 to 1981, of thirty-five years. The seventh cycle began in 1981, when interest rates were at historic, all-time highs, and the trend was downward for thirty-nine years, which I believe ended in 2020. We had a neighbor in Seattle who began his career as a financial advisor in 1980, and he retired after a fulfilling forty-year career. His timing for entering the investment world couldn't have been better. Now, however, we may be in the early stages of a thirty-year uptrend in interest rates, which will not be as favorable for financial assets, such as stocks and bonds."

"Your two-hundred-year perspective is helpful," Pastor Staley said. "I'm surprised interest-rate cycles last so long."

"The second remarkable phenomenon about investing I've discovered has been the seasonality of the US stock market. You've probably heard the saying, 'Sell in May and walk away.' That statement has some basis in fact. There's no question, since 1950, that the November-through-April period has provided substantially better returns than the May-through-October period. In fact, if an investor had taken his or her money out of the stock market in May for six months, the return for being in the stock market for only six months, from November to April, would have been almost the same. This information won't necessarily help a long-term investor because converting stocks to cash for six months each year can be an expensive strategy. Since there can be significant stock-market corrections in the fall, that may be a good time to find attractive investments before a November to April uptrend."

"Is there an explanation for the seasonality?"

"I haven't read a good explanation for it," Matt replied. "The third major observation I'll share is that there has been a sharp decline in the number of listed or publicly traded stocks in the US since 1995. From 1975 to 1995, there was a steady increase of listed companies. Mergers and acquisitions are the major reason for the reduction in listed stocks since 1995. As a result, industries are more concentrated, and the average publicly traded company is larger, older, more profitable, and more likely to pay dividends, according to my reading. If you believe in the concept of supply and demand, the demand for the stocks, given today's smaller supply compared to twenty-five years ago, may continue to push their prices higher over the long term if there's a favorable interest-rate environment."

"When can we get started?" Staley said, chuckling. "I'd like to become an investor!"

"We need to identify thirty to thirty-five high-quality, established US companies with stocks that pay a quarterly dividend. Companies with a long history of paying and growing their dividends have a successful business model that can give us confidence in their future success."

"Can you help me develop a list?" Staley asked.

"Sure. They'll be companies with a history of steady sales and earnings growth, dividend growth, and strong balance sheets with relatively little debt. I try to follow insider purchases, where officers and directors are purchasing shares of their companies because, in theory, they should know better than anyone the value of their companies in relation to their stock prices. A cluster of insider purchases is often a sign that a company's stock is undervalued."

"Are there any other signals you follow?"

"Yes. New product introductions can act as catalysts to boost stock prices," Matt said. "If the market believes a new product will contribute meaningfully to a company's sales and earnings, then investors may be drawn to the stock, and new stock purchases will push it higher."

"Can you give me an example of a catalyst?" Staley asked.

"Sure. Pharmaceutical companies can introduce a new drug," Matt said, "and that news can attract new investors. Also, announcements by a company that it is repurchasing its stock can be a sign that senior management and the board believe their company's stock is undervalued. That news can attract investors. Shrinking the number of shares outstanding increases the ownership percentage of existing shareholders, which is a positive. Finally, a stock split can be viewed as a shareholder-friendly proposal. Stock splits don't change the value of a stock. When the share price is halved, the number of shares is doubled. However, it's a positive development psychologically because investors would rather buy one hundred shares of a stock at fifty dollars per share than fifty shares of a stock at one hundred dollars per share."

"Your presentation has been very interesting and helpful, Matt. I like your approach. Starting a program now will help me develop a plan for investing more money when my parents' house is sold. How do I pay you for your good counsel?"

"I enjoy the investment world, Pastor Staley," Matt said, "and helping you with your investment program will be payment enough. Plus, I'll learn some new things along the way in working with you that will help Jancy and me with our own investments."

"Thank you for your offer, but I'll figure out a way to incorporate your investment help into the income you receive as a trustee of our family trust," Staley said. "I'd also like to return to your office at two o'clock in two weeks after I open an investment account and deposit the money with a brokerage firm. Then we can discuss your stock recommendations for our initial investments."

"That's a good plan," Matt said. "I'll try to have the names of thirty or thirty-five companies to present to you. You might consider initially investing ten thousand dollars in ten of them and adding fifteen over the next two years. That would mean your $250,000 investment account might eventually own twenty-five stocks. When you have more funds, you can increase your holdings to thirty or thirty-five names. Before you leave, here's a list of a few investment observations I made over the weekend, using the first ten letters in the alphabet. Maybe we can discuss them at our next meeting, as well. I look forward to our next conversation."

Staley looked at the list and read them out loud: "A—Avoid the herd mentality. B—Buybacks of shares by companies increase ownership percentages. C—Cash on the balance sheet gives a company positive options. D—Dividends and their annual growth matter to investors seeking income. E—Earnings growth propels stock prices.

F—Fewer stock sales will reduce expenses and tax consequences. G—Great companies are few and far between. H—Heavy debt can weigh on a company's profitability. I—Insider buys can indicate an undervalued stock. J—Judge a company by its track record. I'll think about these concepts over the next two weeks," Staley said. "Let's discuss them at our next meeting. I've enjoyed our conversation." Staley gathered his notes and left Matt's office.

# 13

MATT CONTINUED TO LEARN about the Dead Sea Scrolls. He explored the subject on his computer, reading about their discovery in the Qumran caves in 1947, as well as uncovering more contemporary information that fraudulent scroll fragments had been offered for sale in the past two decades. Placing a telephone call to his Old Testament professor at Calvin Seminary, Matt obtained the names of several books and articles to read. The professor was aware of Pastor Staley's inheritance. He also knew that Matt had taken a ministerial position at Hacienda Presbyterian and invited him to make a presentation on the Dead Sea Scrolls to his seminary class in the fall.

A recurring subject in Matt's research was the Maamoun family in Bethlehem who had been involved in buying and selling scrolls from the beginning. Matt wanted to speak to Michael Maamoun, the son of the patriarch, to discover if he knew about another Esther Scroll, either in his possession or owned by a private investor. If Maamoun did not know of another, Matt would have more confidence in Staley's scroll being a one-of-a-kind. The more he knew about the Dead Sea Scrolls, and the Esther Scroll in particular, the better he could gauge its importance and value.

Eventually, Matt asked Staley if he would fund a weekend trip for Matt to visit Israel to meet in person with Michael Maamoun, whose father had received from a Bedouin the first seven scrolls discovered in the Qumran caves. After thinking about it for a day, Staley agreed to pay for the trip if Matt could obtain an appointment with Maamoun.

Matt wrote a letter to Maamoun and, within two weeks, received a return message that proposed a couple of appointment dates. After showing Maamoun's e-mail to Pastor Staley, Matt was given approval to book his flight. He confirmed his meeting with Maamoun with an e-mail and scheduled a late-afternoon flight on Thursday on El Al Israel Airlines, the national airline and flag carrier of Israel. Departing from San Francisco International flight, he would arrive at Ben Gurion International Airport in Lod, Israel, and return the following Tuesday. The departing twelve-hour flight would provide an opportunity to sleep during the night and put him in Israel the next afternoon, around one thirty.

Jancy drove Matt to the San Francisco International Airport. After a long embrace, Matt took his suitcase from the back seat and walked into the airport, ready to start his adventure. He checked his suitcase at the El Al counter, passed through security, and used the moving sidewalks to find his way to the departure terminal, which was located a good distance from the central terminal. While he waited to board the Boeing 787-9 Dreamliner, he worked a *New York Times* crossword puzzle.

El Al employees circulated among the passengers, asking questions. "Why are you traveling to Israel?" and "Are you traveling alone?" It appeared the airline was concerned about knowing who was traveling to Israel and why.

The plane was full. Passengers, mostly American tourists, were a mix of people, including observant Jews and Orthodox Jews. Observant male Jews wore kippahs, brimless cloth skullcaps, and tassels on their waists, while the women covered their hair with scarves, hats, or berets. The Orthodox male Jews wore white shirts and long, black coats, as well as black pants and tall black hats. The Orthodox Jewish women also wore dark clothing—dresses or skirts with shirts or blouses that covered their arms.

The flight to Israel was calm and trouble free. Matt tried to sleep but was only marginally successful. Late at night, he was aware that the Orthodox Jews gathered in the back of the plane for a kind of worship that involved wrapping their arms with black bands and repeating prayers out loud.

Thirty minutes before the plane's arrival, a flight attendant told the passengers, first in Hebrew and then in English, to turn off their cell phones and use the restroom if necessary. As the plane began its descent into the Ben Gurion Airport, passengers were asked to remain in their seats, and the window covers were lowered. This precaution caused conversations to stop, and the cabin became quiet. They were entering a nation that faced security dangers every day, and that reality registered with the passengers as the plane prepared to land. Matt wondered if lowering the window covers was for security purposes, so that photos and videos of Israel couldn't be taken as the plane began its decline toward the airport.

Arriving shortly after one-thirty in the afternoon, Matt disembarked and walked toward the baggage claim area. He first had to be screened at a passport control post, so he joined one of the lanes to have his passport inspected. When he came to the woman sitting behind a glass window, she stared at him for several seconds and then appeared to look at a screen filled with information about him. She asked Matt if he was traveling alone, which he affirmed. Matt was coached to ask for an entry permit, rather than having his passport stamped. He was told that an Israeli stamp on his passport might make traveling to other Middle Eastern countries more difficult in the future. Once he received the paper entry permit with his photo on it and passed through the turnstile ahead of him, he was officially in Israel. He proceeded to the large baggage claim area, where he saw luggage, backpacks, crates, and packages from all over the world delivered to eleven carousels in the busy airport. Finding his suitcase on the designated carousel, Matt walked outside to locate the van from the Ambassador Hotel. It was already after two o'clock. He was surprised by the bright sunlight, which made him pause for a few moments on the sidewalk. The intensity of the sun's rays was similar to what he experienced on visits to Texas.

Matt had reserved a room at Jerusalem's Ambassador Hotel and arranged through the concierge to be picked up at the airport by a hotel van. The ride from the airport to the hotel in East Jerusalem took about forty-five minutes. Matt was impressed with the attractive, contemporary, and understated appearance of the six-story hotel with its tan, sandstone façade. The hotel was located on a hill in an Arab neighborhood with spectacular views of the surrounding city.

He entered the hotel, received his room key at the front desk, and went to his room for a short nap. Later, refreshed, he walked around the attractive grounds. In a barren land, the property seemed like an oasis. Lush vegetation, including shrubs and small trees, blended with grass and numerous palm trees.

That evening, after many hours of traveling, Matt was ready for dinner. The hotel dining room offered a buffet with a salad table, entrée table, and dessert table. He filled his salad plate with a good selection of vegetables and chose a white fish, tilapia, for his entrée. The fish is thought to be the kind caught by St. Peter in the Sea of Galilee and fed by Jesus to the masses during his ministry. For dessert, Matt chose several pieces of almond bread, which had been baked twice, and he ordered an espresso. After dinner, he took another stroll around the grounds to get some fresh air before retiring early. He wanted to be well rested for his ten thirty meeting with Michael Maamoun.

Breakfast the next morning included peach yogurt, scrambled eggs, and a selection of breads. Matt took a taxi to the Maamoun souvenir shop in Bethlehem. A line of cars at the check point delayed the taxi's entrance into the West Bank by a half-hour. It took another half-hour to reach Maamoun's store. Matt arrived at the store in a well-maintained building and, after paying the taxi driver, crossed the sidewalk and entered through a glass door. Inside, a variety of religious artifacts and jewelry were for sale, and the store was full of tourists. He told a clerk he had an appointment with Michael Maamoun and was taken to a back office.

Maamoun greeted Matt with a smile and invited him into his large but windowless office. Maamoun was medium height, with black hair and mustache, and wore light brown slacks, a blue Polo shirt, and a tan windbreaker. "Welcome to Bethlehem and the West Bank, Reverend Beringer. How was your flight to Israel?"

"Very smooth and comfortable. It may take me a while to adjust to the change in time zones."

"Can I offer you some Turkish coffee or a cold glass of sparkling lemonade?"

"Yes. A cold lemonade would be perfect," Matt replied.

Maamoun told the clerk, who had been waiting at the door, to bring two glasses of lemonade. Then Maamoun settled into a chair behind a desk and offered a chair to Matt. "Since you've become a trustee of the Staley Family Trust, you're now involved with the Esther Scroll. Has Pastor Staley decided what he wants to do with it?" Maamoun wasted no time in revealing an interest in the scroll.

"He has no immediate plans," Matt said, "but there may be a sale sometime in the future."

"Very interesting. We would like to discuss the possibility of acquiring the Esther Scroll, so put us on your list and contact us when that day arrives."

"I will do that," Matt said, opening his notebook on his lap. "Thank you for taking the time to meet with me. I'm trying to learn as much as I can about the Dead Sea Scrolls. Since your family has played a significant role in their history, I thought a conversation with you would be an important step in my research. Could you tell me a little about your family's involvement with the scrolls?"

"With pleasure. A handful of Bedouin shepherds found the first seven scrolls in the Qumran caves, probably in early 1947, and took them to my father, who worked with leather, making and repairing shoes. My father recognized the scrolls were made from untanned animal hides or parchment. As the Bedouin searched for buyers for the seven scrolls, they became separated. Three were acquired for the Hebrew University in Jerusalem by Professor E. L. Sukenik, who bought them from a Bethlehem antiquities dealer, Faidi Salahi. My father acquired and sold the remaining four scrolls to Archbishop Mar Samuel of the Syriac Orthodox Church in Jerusalem for around a hundred dollars. He kept a third of that payment and gave the rest to the Bedouin who found them."

Maamoun continued, "Archbishop Samuel took the four scrolls to the United States and later sold them through an ad in the *Wall Street Journal* on June 11, 1954. They were acquired through some trickery by Yigael Yadin, the son of Professor Sukenik. As a result of working with those original seven scrolls from Cave 1, my father became an antiquities dealer in 1952. During the 1950s and 1960s, he was the established negotiator for the Bedouin. From dealing with numerous scrolls and other artifacts, my father became an icon in the antiquities market. Those seven scrolls are now housed together at the Shrine of the Book, a wing of the Israel Museum in Jerusalem. I think you would enjoy seeing the scrolls at the museum."

"I've read," Matt said, "that Archbishop Samuel is reported to have taken fragments of Daniel and Enoch, along with the Prayer Scroll, when he left Jerusalem. I suppose he could have taken many other fragments, as well."

"You may be right," Maamoun said. "My family believes the four scrolls that Archbishop Samuel took to the United States and sold to Yadin belong to us. We have papers that give us a mortgage on the St. Mark's monastery property in Jerusalem. However, because we are Syriac Christians, we're not interested in taking legal action against our own church."

"I've read extensively about those seven scrolls," Matt said, looking at his notebook. "There was the twenty-four-foot-long Isaiah Scroll; the Habakkuk Commentary; the Manual of Discipline, which was in two pieces; and the Genesis Apocryphon, all of which were acquired by Archbishop Samuel and later sold to Yigael Yadin. Professor Sukenik acquired the second Isaiah Scroll, the War Scroll, and the Thanksgiving Scroll. Beyond these scrolls, your father sold other Cave 1 fragments to G. L. Harding, director of Antiquities for Jordan, and Roland de Vaux, president of the Palestine Archaeological Museum in Jerusalem."

"That's right. Those men deserve a lot of credit for acquiring and preserving the scrolls for posterity."

"Finding Caves 2 through 11 in the early 1950s generated so many fragments," Matt continued. "I've read that over fifteen thousand scroll fragments have been found in the eleven caves, and 60 percent of them came from Cave 4. Harding and de Vaux assembled a team of eight scholars to identify, sort, and reconstruct those fragments from Cave 4 and prepare them for publication. That was a huge project."

"I agree," Maamoun said. "The number of discoveries has been remarkable. My family has been at the right place at the right time, you might say. We've done well as an antiquities dealer, and we have a good reputation in the business. There have been a wide variety of scrolls found, biblical and non-biblical, including the famous Copper Scroll."

"It's been described as a treasure map," Matt said, "with sixty-four places where large amounts of gold and silver are buried."

"We'll probably never know who owned the treasure," Maamoun said, "if it existed at all. It seems likely the scroll belonged to the ascetic Essenes at Qumran. Maybe it referred to temple treasure, hidden before the destruction of the Jerusalem Temple in 70 CE. It's a mystery that remains to be solved."

"I've read," Matt said, "that the Cave 4 discoveries are more important than even the original seven scrolls. Many Old Testament books were found there, and about 75 percent of the Old Testament is represented by that massive find."

"Yes," Maamoun said with raised eyebrows, seemingly impressed with Matt's extensive knowledge. "While de Vaux was excavating Qumran, the Bedouin were busy searching the caves for more treasures."

"I found it interesting," Matt said, "that Harding and de Vaux, at first, would pay for each item presented to them. However, over time, that arrangement changed. The officials at the Museum—Harding, de Vaux, and Saad—realized the Bedouin were tearing up fragments into smaller pieces to increase the total price. The amount paid was adjusted to a fixed price. An inscribed fragment was valued at one pound sterling per square centimeter."

"It was a smart move for the museum because funds were very limited in those days," Maamoun said, "and the number of fragments was growing, especially after the Cave 4 artifacts were acquired."

"I'm kind of a numbers guy," Matt said, referring to his notes. "Your father was paid $97.20 for the four scrolls he sold to Archbishop Samuel. In 1953, Harding paid $42,000 for Cave 4 fragments on behalf of the Jordanian government. An amount of $44,800 was paid to your father by de Vaux at the museum on March 1, 1956, for eight cardboard boxes and one package of Cave 11 fragments. All told, I've read that the museum paid a total of around $184,000 for the purchase of scrolls between 1950 and 1958."

"I'm impressed by your research," Maamoun said.

"Thank you," Matt said. "I've only just begun, and I'm up to about 1960 in reading about the scroll discoveries."

"You're off to a good start. The Dead Sea Scrolls are an important subject to study."

"There has been some discussion about the nature of the Qumran community," Matt said. "The consensus seems to be that it was a monastic community of men who were regular practitioners of daily immersion. There has been conversation about whether the scrolls came from the Qumran community or if they were brought to Qumran from Jerusalem or elsewhere. However, there were blank pieces of parchment found in Caves 4 and 5, which proved to some scholars that scrolls were copied at Qumran. Otherwise, why would there have been blank parchments there?"

"There have also been some scribal tables and ink wells discovered among the ruins at Qumran," Maamoun said, "which provide additional support to the argument that scribes worked there and that some of the scrolls were written there."

"The Samuel Scroll found in Cave 4," Matt continued, "is the oldest of the manuscripts recovered from Qumran, estimated to date as far back as the mid-third century BCE or even earlier. One of the team members said he believed the fragments of Samuel made it the best represented biblical manuscript in the scroll collection from Cave 4."

"You may be correct," Maamoun said. "It is thought that many of the scrolls came from other communities beyond the Essene community, such as from the Jerusalem Temple. In addition, ancient coins have been found at Qumran from all over the Mediterranean."

"I've profiled the team of eight scholars that Harding and de Vaux assembled in the early 1950s to work on the fragments from Cave 4: Cross, Milik, Allegro, Starcky, Strugnell, Hunzinger, Skehan, and Baillet. They were a diverse and committed group, drawn primarily from Europe."

"My father knew them all," Maamoun said.

"One of them had an alcohol problem," Matt said, "which included periods of excessive drinking, accompanied by work powered largely by coffee and cigarettes. A few of the men were reserved and shy, and some were more productive than others. One of them felt the scroll fragments he was given were 'leftovers,' but this may have been because, as a New Testament specialist, he was not very proficient in Hebrew. Some were better than others in analyzing ancient writing systems and dating the manuscripts, while others were stronger in understanding ancient languages. For the most part, they were a diverse and congenial group, but I did uncover a maverick."

"I'll bet I know who that was," Maamoun said, smiling. "My father's least favorite of the group was John Allegro. He described my father as a 'cobbler,' and that offended him."

"Yes," Matt said. "Allegro appears to have been an interesting team member, and I've read a fair amount about him and his focus on the Copper Scroll. He was the only agnostic among them. Several persons had explored how to open the scroll, which was found in two pieces. Allegro worked with the School of Technology, associated with the University of Manchester, where the scroll was finally cut open by Professor Wright Baker in 1955. Allegro was excited to begin the transcription and translation of the Copper Scroll. He published an article in *Time* magazine on February 6, 1956, titled "Crucifixion before Christ," based on his analysis that a 'Teacher of Righteousness' cited in the scroll might have been crucified. Allegro's assertions troubled Harding, and members of the team took exception to Allegro's interpretations. Described as an extrovert by his wife, Allegro approached the BBC about sharing the message of the Copper Scroll, but these efforts to publicize the Dead Sea Scrolls on BBC radio broadcasts were not well received by Harding, who felt Allegro had violated protocols regulating the work of the team."

"Allegro's effort to promote his own work drew worldwide attention to the Dead Sea Scrolls," Maamoun said, "and not all of it was positive."

"Allegro's Team 4 members," Matt said, "rejected his line of reasoning, not for theological reasons but for linguistic reasons. In 1956, a letter rejecting some of Allegro's claims, signed by de Vaux and four members of the Cave 4 Team, appeared in the London *Times*. Later in his life, Allegro, the only non-Christian in the group, moved farther away from Christian orthodoxy. One of his books, *The Sacred Mushroom and the Cross*, published in 1970, suggests the stories in the New Testament were intended to convey the rites and rules of mushroom worship to believers."

"Allegro was a colorful character," Maamoun said, "and his interpretations from his scroll work differed greatly from the conclusions of his other team members."

Matt added, "He certainly enlivened the history of scroll work being conducted at the museum in the 1950s!"

"As you know," Maamoun said, "some Old Testament books have been found in greater abundance than others. Among all the scrolls discovered, there have been thirty-nine copies of Psalms, thirty-three copies of Deuteronomy, twenty-four of Genesis, and twenty-two of Isaiah. The Dead Sea Scrolls have been a rich source of historical, religious, and linguistic information for the past seventy-plus years. The twenty-four-foot-long Isaiah Scroll at the Shrine of the Book is especially impressive. If my family had been able to retain that scroll, among others, I probably wouldn't be here speaking with you today. I'd be on a beach in the south of France," he said, smiling.

After their wide-ranging discussion of the Dead Sea Scrolls, Matt thought it was time to shift the conversation to the missing link that Staley had inherited. "Can I assume, then, that you've never seen an Esther scroll?" Matt asked.

"I'm not able to give you a definitive answer," Maamoun said, stroking his mustache. "All I will say is, if we own an Esther fragment, we would also be very receptive to owning a second one."

*If Maamoun owned a fragment of the Esther Scroll, I would think he'd want the world to know it*, Matt thought. *Maybe someone would make an offer for it that he couldn't refuse.* Matt wanted to keep Maamoun's focus on the Esther Scroll. "Why haven't we heard about one being found in the caves?"

"I don't think it was a popular book among the Essenes who lived at Qumran. The fact that the book of Esther doesn't mention God in the narrative made it unappealing to the community. However, that doesn't mean there aren't some Esther scrolls in existence. They just haven't been publicized."

"Could there be some additional reasons why the book of Esther may not have been very popular in the Essene community? Part of it could be that the heroine in Esther is a Jewish girl who marries a Persian king and that the story occurs in a Persian court."

"I prefer to stay with my first answer. The story doesn't mention God."

"Okay. Just out of curiosity, are you offering any fragments of the Dead Sea Scrolls for sale at the present time?"

"Our store offers moderately priced religious artifacts and jewelry to tourists, but occasionally we have a wealthy investor who is interested in owning a scroll fragment. We have a library of fragments in a vault that we can discuss with the right kind of buyer."

"If I may ask, what do your more expensive fragments cost?"

"We're usually starting at five hundred thousand dollars or more, depending upon the size, quality, and book involved. For example, a fragment of Isaiah would be worth more than a fragment of a lesser-known book."

"We're in the process of having the Esther Scroll appraised. What kind of price would you place on it?"

"Before I set a price, I'd have to see it. However, I would think it would be safe to say the price would be in excess of a million dollars."

"Buying and selling scroll fragments these days appears to be a complicated business. Sadly, I've read that some transactions over the past two decades have involved fraudulent scroll fragments, but we can leave that subject for another conversation."

"Buyers need to be careful when purchasing scroll fragments. Doing business with a reputable dealer is most important."

"I've also read about some recent scroll discoveries," Matt said, pulling an article from his notebook. "In 2017, Israeli archaeologists found twenty-four fragments from a scroll written in Greek, which they believe dates from the First Temple period, from 950 to 586 BCE. They also found some coins from the same period. Discoveries continue to be found in the Qumran."

"They also found a woven basket that's been dated to around 10,500 years ago," Maamoun said, "making it the world's oldest basket. A mummy of a young girl, with an estimated age of six to twelve, was also discovered. It's been dated to about six thousand years ago. These are remarkable findings. They were well preserved because of the dry climate of the caves."

Their conversation continued for another fifteen minutes. Maamoun asked Matt what sights he had seen on his visit. He was curious to know if the Dead Sea Scrolls were being studied in US seminaries and repeated his interest in acquiring the Esther Scroll if Staley decided to sell it. And he also asked how many others had wanted to buy the scroll.

During their meeting, they had discussed the topics Matt had hoped to review, but he was frustrated Maamoun wouldn't confirm or deny knowledge of another Esther Scroll. Clearly, Maamoun kept things close to his vest. Perhaps part of his family's success in the antiquities business had been knowing how to keep secrets.

Matt's visit with Maamoun wasn't as productive as he had expected it would be. He hoped Maamoun didn't recognize the disappointment he was feeling as he concluded their conversation. Matt thanked Maamoun for his hospitality, shook his hand, and left the store.

Once outside, he began walking toward his next destination: the nearby Church of the Nativity. Matt had an interest in visiting the church because it's considered the birthplace of Jesus. The grotto within the basilica is the oldest site continuously used as a place of worship in Christianity, and the building is the oldest major church in the Holy Land. Scholars agree that a wooden stable or manger was an unlikely setting for Jesus's birth, compared to a location in a cave, due to the abundance of rock formations and the scarcity of wood in the Bethlehem area. Houses would have been built in front of a cave, which would have been used for stabling and storage. Therefore, Jesus's birth in a cave or stone grotto makes sense. The precise location of Jesus's birth was first identified by St. Justin Martyr in 160 CE, and the place for a church was chosen by Constantine's mother, Helena, who visited the site from 325 to 326 CE. The basilica, dedicated in 339 CE, was built under the guidance of Helena and commissioned by Constantine, who became a Christian himself and legalized Christianity in the Roman Empire.

Matt walked across a large parking lot to join the crowd of tourists standing at the entrance to the ancient Byzantine church. Its tiny entrance was dwarfed by the building's massive size, covering almost 130,000 square feet and including three different monasteries—Greek Orthodox, Armenian Apostolic, and Roman Catholic.

Around 1500, Christians reduced the size of the original opening to prevent Ottoman thieves from riding horses into the sanctuary and looting the church. Given his height, Matt had to stoop low at the Door of Humility and get on his knees and crawl over the raised threshold through the entrance to the church, which he estimated was a little over four feet high and three feet wide. Once inside the two-foot-thick wall, he waited in a line of tourists before descending the stairs to see the enclosed grotto with a silver star, surrounded by candles, marking the place where Christ was born. Matt was able to bend down and touch the fourteen-pointed silver star, whose points represent the fourteen generations from Abraham to David, fourteen generations from David until the Babylonian exile, and fourteen generations between the Babylonian exile until the Messiah.

After his visit to the Church of the Nativity, Matt caught a taxi for the trip back to the Ambassador Hotel. He took a short nap and then ventured into the dining room because he was hungry and hadn't eaten since morning. After dinner, he walked around the grounds to get some exercise before going to bed. Tomorrow, he would buy something to take home to Jancy.

———•———

For breakfast, served once again in buffet style, Matt enjoyed a dish called *shakshouka*, a Maghrebi dish of eggs poached in a sauce of tomatoes, olive oil, peppers, onion, and garlic, spiced with cumin, paprika, cayenne pepper, and nutmeg. He followed that with a piece of lemon-blackberry coffee cake. After a cup of coffee, Matt took a taxi to view the Western Wall.

The ancient limestone structure is the holiest place where Jews can pray because the most sacred site in the Jewish faith, the Holy of Holies—the inner sanctuary of the Temple Mount—lies behind it. The wall measures 160 feet in length and sixty feet high, and it is part of a much longer retaining wall originally built as part of the expansion of the Second Temple of Jerusalem. Construction of the wall may have been started by Herod the Great in 19 BCE. An almost rectangular set of retaining walls was constructed to support an expansion of the hill, or Temple Mount, above the walls, on which a large, paved platform was added that surrounds the temple.

Matt entered the large plaza and walked to the Western Wall, which is part of a 1,601-foot retaining wall on the western side of the Temple Mount. The plaza was full of tourists and Jews who were praying. Before approaching the wall, Matt took a kippah from a table to cover his head. Then he walked down a ramp to the men's area for prayer in front of the wall. Matt had written a prayer on a piece of paper, which he folded and inserted into one of the crevices. People were sitting in chairs and praying close to the wall. Many, mainly Jews in their religious apparel, stood praying next to the wall, some touching it with their hands and others with their foreheads leaning against it. After standing in front of the wall for several minutes, Matt found a chair near the divider that separates the men's prayer area from that for the women. For Orthodox Jews, men and women are prohibited from praying together. He sat in the chair for at least an hour, reading and thinking about his favorite Bible verses, which he kept on his cell phone, and watching men of all shapes and sizes, wearing everything from sweatshirts to business suits, come and go from prayer in front of the Western Wall. All of them wore kippahs.

Returning to the Ambassador Hotel for lunch, Matt then called for a taxi to make another trip to Bethlehem, this time to the Three Arches, a jewelry store that had been recommended to him. Owned by the same family since the early 1600s, the business of designing and manufacturing jewelry had been passed down from generation to generation. The Three Arches company was established in 1853 and is currently managed by a family member. The taxi delivered Matt to 388 Manger Street, and inside the large store, Matt found shelves full of souvenirs. The store specialized in olive wood products, as well as jewelry, Bibles, mother of pearl objects, Nativity sets, and crosses. He was thinking about buying Jancy a necklace with a Jerusalem cross, decorated with gemstones. After a half-hour of looking, he found the item he wanted. He spent twice what he had planned because he found a necklace with a Jerusalem cross pendant that had a small diamond in each quadrant. The cost somehow wasn't important to him compared to the memory it would provide. He didn't know when he would be returning to Israel, and he wanted Jancy to know how special she was to him. After he made his purchase, he returned to the Ambassador for the night. Tomorrow, Monday, he had other important places to visit.

———————◆———————

Matt was excited about visiting Qumran, site of the Essene community near the Dead Sea and the area where the Dead Sea Scrolls were discovered in caves. He had arranged to join a guided tour, and the bus would pick him up at eight in the morning. He chose an early morning tour because he wanted to complete his trip by noon to avoid the afternoon heat. In a small pouch that hung from a strap around his neck, Matt carried a bottle of water that would keep him hydrated. The bus ride through barren terrain to Qumran National Park was completed in just under an hour. Upon arriving, he and a busload of tourists watched a short introductory film in a building at the entrance. Then they proceeded to the excavation where the Essenes once lived. At the site, archaeologists had uncovered a scriptorium, a room devoted to copying religious texts. Structures thought to be writing benches with inkwells were identified by the tour guide. The dig had also discovered pieces of pottery in the scriptorium that were the same as the pottery found in the caves with the Dead Sea Scrolls. These findings confirm that at least some of the scrolls came from the Essene library. Other scholars believe that many of the scrolls came from the Jerusalem Temple, brought there just before the siege of Jerusalem by the Romans in 70 CE.

One of the most interesting features of the excavation, from Matt's perspective, was the dining room where the Essenes ate their communal meals. Over one thousand serving vessels have been found, including plates, cups, and bowls. He was also intrigued by the ancient aqueduct that brought water to the Essene community. The water from the Qumran Stream and the Eynot Stream provided the essential drinking water the community needed for everyday use and to irrigate nearby land and raise animals. The water was channeled into cisterns that were used for a variety of purposes. It is thought the community members used water to perform daily cleansing rituals. From the excavation site, Matt was also able to view a few of the caves on the hillside where the Dead Sea Scrolls had been discovered.

After spending over an hour touring the Qumran National Park, Matt and the other tour members boarded the bus and returned to the Ambassador Hotel, arriving just before noon. He was tired from his morning activities, but he wanted to visit the Church of the Holy Sepulchre in the Old City before calling it a day. Matt didn't want to leave Jerusalem without visiting the church that included the two holiest sites in Christianity: the place where Jesus was crucified, called Calvary or Golgotha, and the location of Jesus's empty tomb. He took a brief ride in a taxi to the Damascus Gate.

Once he was inside the Old City, in the Christian Quarter, Matt felt hungry and decided to find something to eat. Someone at the Ambassador had recommended he try a falafel sandwich, so he spotted a storefront restaurant that was preparing sandwiches. Matt watched a person behind the window holding a pita pocket in his left hand. From containers on the counter in front of him, he deftly added ingredients to make the sandwich. First, he selected several falafel balls made of a beef and lamb mixture. From another container, he ladled a large spoonful of the blend of tomato, cucumber, onion, and parsley. The sandwich was topped off with a creamy white sauce made from a sesame seed paste. The man handed the sandwich to Matt through the doorway and took his payment. Matt also bought a cold bottle of soda and found a place to sit and enjoy the delicious sandwich.

After lunch, Matt approached the entrance to the church from the south, crossing a crowded courtyard. The massive stone building is not the original one constructed by Constantine in the fourth century, but it is a structure that was rebuilt in the twelfth century. Matt faced two large Gothic doorways, but since the one on the right had been filled with a stone wall, he entered the church through the double doors of the left portal. Once inside, he turned right and ascended a series of steep stairs. Reaching the second level, Matt encountered a series of small worship spaces that comprise over thirty chapels and worship sites within the church. The chapels depict the Stations of the Cross, showing Jesus nailed to the cross, dying on the cross, and being taken down from the cross. In the first chapel, he could see the top of Golgotha under glass. Also, a silver disc beneath an altar signified the place where it is thought the cross stood. Returning to the main floor, Matt entered the church's rotunda, featuring huge pillars and a large dome. In the center was a small shrine, which contained the tomb of Christ, where he rose from the dead after three days. Matt learned that three denominations share ownership of the church: Greek Orthodox Church, Roman Catholic Church, and Armenian Orthodox Church. Three minor Orthodox communities, Coptic, Syriac, and Ethiopian, have rights to use certain areas. The terms of this arrangement were delineated in the Status Quo, a collection of laws, rules, and historical traditions instituted by the Ottoman sultan Osman III in 1757. Matt also thought it was curious that after Salah A-din recaptured

Jerusalem in 1192, he assigned the responsibility of opening the church doors to two Muslim families, one to serve as a key keeper and the other to use the key to open the door, and members of the two families have continued to open the doors for over eight hundred years.

Tired from his long day, Matt returned to the Ambassador Hotel to take a nap before dinner. It was a short taxi ride back to the hotel, where Matt was grateful to be able to lie down and finally get off his feet.

———•———

AFTER BREAKFAST THE NEXT MORNING, Matt wanted to spend several more hours exploring the Old City. While there were other places in Israel that he wanted to see, such as the Church of Saint Catherine in Bethlehem, Matt had run out of time. He also would have enjoyed taking the two-and-a-half-hour bus ride to the Sea of Galilee so he could have visited Capernaum and seen the area where Jesus had conducted much of his ministry. However, those sights and more would have to wait for another visit.

He took a taxi, once again, to the Damascus Gate. It is the largest and most impressive of the gates to the Old City. Flanked on either side by towers, the structure was a gate built during the Ottoman rule of Suleiman the Magnificent in 1537. Beneath the gate were remains of an earlier gate, dating back to the time of the Roman Emperor Hadrian in the second century CE. On top of the gate was a parapet, or low wall, with pointed merlons running along the top, allowing for spaces of crenellations in between for defenders to shoot cannons or use other weapons.

Matt spent the next three hours walking through the Old City on a self-guided tour. While touring its narrow passageways, Matt began to absorb the culture of Jerusalem. Composed of many narrow streets and alleys, it is full of shops where almost everything can be found. He savored exotic smells emanating from the flower shops and spice stores. Venders offered a wide spectrum of items, including fruits and vegetables, clothing, kitchenware, shoes, and a variety of meats. Part of the street noise came from shoppers negotiating with venders over what they wanted to buy.

The streets were full of people, competing for limited space with carts, bicycles, and specially sized vehicles. Occasionally, he would detour into interesting alleyways. Several times he was bumped by persons going other directions. On his walk, he saw at least two groups of small boys, and he was told they work together, using the strategy of distraction, to pickpocket tourists. He was glad he wore a money belt under his shirt to protect his valuables, including his cash and credit cards. After completing his tour, Matt was ready to return to the Ambassador. He took a taxi to the hotel and relaxed for a few hours before dinner. Afterwards, he packed his suitcase for his midnight departure from the Ben Gurion Airport. As he sat on the edge of the bed, he began to feel weary. He realized he had been running on adrenalin most of the weekend, taking in as many sights of the ancient land as he could in a short period.

He boarded the hotel van at eight o'clock, giving him plenty of time to reach the airport about an hour and a half before the flight. Entering the airport, he stood in line for an initial security check. Matt encountered El Al employees who asked him numerous questions, such as "Where have you traveled?" and "Has anyone given you anything?" and "Did you pack your own suitcase?" Then Matt checked his suitcase at the El Al counter. At a second security check, he passed through a metal detector and then began his long walk to the departure terminal.

Once on board the plane, Matt settled into his seat for the long flight home. It felt good to relax after maintaining a very full schedule in Israel. His visit with Michael Maamoun had been interesting, but he wasn't able to confirm that Pastor Staley owned the only Esther Scroll. Matt had gained a much greater appreciation of Jewish and Christian history by visiting some of the major religious sites in Jerusalem. What stories he would have to share with Jancy, Pastor Staley, and the Hacienda staff upon his return to the East Bay. And, for Jancy, he carried a gift that would be a lasting memory of his visit to the ancient land.

# 14

Matt was happy to be home from his trip to Israel. Jancy was thrilled with her necklace, and he enjoyed telling her about all the people he had met and the places he had seen. She was captivated by the photos he had taken.

On his second day in the office, Matt had met with Pastor Staley and made the rounds of Hacienda staff to tell them about his adventures. His meeting with Pastor Staley was not as upbeat as he had hoped it would be. Matt was uncomfortable because he had gained little from his meeting with Michael Maamoun. While his trip was personally enjoyable because of the important places he had visited, Matt had no new information to share about the Esther Scroll. Gathering fresh information about the scroll was the purpose of the trip, and he had returned empty-handed. Maamoun's willingness to share his knowledge about the Esther Scroll had not matched his hospitality. Matt had returned with nothing that would help Staley better evaluate the worth of the Esther Scroll and confirm that it was the only such scroll in existence. Because Matt considered the trip to be a failure, he offered to repay Staley for at least half of the cost, but he declined. Staley told Matt he suspected Maamoun might not disclose much information during their meeting but felt it was a step they needed to take because of the special association Maamoun's family had with the Dead Sea Scrolls. He said he was grateful Matt had deepened their relationship with Maamoun by meeting with him in person. In addition, Staley said he was not interested in traveling all the way to Israel, and he was relieved Matt had offered to make the trip.

On his third day back, Matt stood in the church office, sipping a cup of coffee. On the counter in front of him, he had placed the contents of his mailbox—a couple of envelopes, a magazine, and the *San Lucas Weekly*.

"Hey, Matt," Mrs. Kirby called as she emerged from behind her glass partition. "I meant to tell you they've hired an assistant for me. She'll help lighten my workload."

"What sob story did you share with Pastor Staley this time?" Matt asked, smiling.

"I've been dropping hints for years! I think he was worried I might quit!"

"Because you know where all the bodies are buried! He may have been concerned you were going to blackmail the church for more money."

"Very funny," she said, "but it has crossed my mind once or twice."

"I've had members tell me that, when they call the church, nobody answers the phone. Finally, we'll have someone who will pick it up."

"I'm going to throw a book at you. You know I have about ten women volunteers who help me with the phones."

"I do, and they do a fabulous job. That's why I knew I could tease you about it."

"Well, don't press your luck, buddy. I'm one of your biggest fans, so you'd better be nice to me."

"You know I enjoy teasing people I like. Thanks for telling me about your new assistant. I knew the Session had approved a new hire, but I didn't know when it was going to happen. This is good news. I'm glad they've found someone," Matt said.

"Only I wish I could have been more involved in her hiring," Mrs. Kirby said. "The applicants were interviewed by a small committee headed by David Marshall. I just interviewed one person, their first choice. The young lady they selected is a little light on experience, but I'm hoping she's a quick learner. It's an entry-level salary, so, as the saying goes, you get what you pay for."

"You can say that again. During college, I had a job one summer in a building in Seattle where the elevators were always being repaired. One day, I asked a guy working on them what the problem was, and he said to me, 'You get what you pay for.' I trust we're paying enough to find the right person for the job. Most of all, I hope you'll enjoy working with her."

"She attended San Lucas High School and just graduated from Cal State East Bay, so I think she's smart enough."

"How'd they find her?"

"David put an ad in the San Lucas and Oakland newspapers," she said, "and he received about fifteen résumés. He and two others spent the last week interviewing about seven of the candidates. I think they were pleased with the quality of the applicants."

"It would have been nice if they had found two or three finalists and given you the opportunity to interview them, so you could have been part of the final decision," Matt said.

"I agree, but David is convinced they selected the best one. Still, I think it's important she and I are on the same page, don't you?"

"Yes, I do. She needs to know what a tyrant you are before she starts."

"She's coming in to complete some forms around one, and I'll take her on a tour of the church. I hope we won't find you shooting baskets in the gym. I want her to think that we do some work around here. It would be nice if she met some of the staff, so would you stop by the office at two o'clock and say hello? I plan to invite Lisa, Pastor Boyle, and Carlo, as well. Pastor Staley has another appointment. We'll have some cold drinks, coffee, and cookies."

"Sounds good. Cookies, did you say? I'll be here."

"Good," Mrs. Kirby said. "I knew I could snag you with some cookies. Thanks for telling Pastor Staley that I needed some help. He told me that you suggested it. I really appreciate it."

"No problem," Matt said. "Glad I could help." As he turned to leave, Matt asked, "What's her first name?"

"Sharon. Her last name is Gray."

"Okay. See you at two."

"One more thing," Mrs. Kirby said.

Matt turned around.

"Sharon and her parents attended Hacienda for a couple of years, maybe five or six years ago, when she was in high school."

"She's an alum, then, you might say."

"It's a little more complicated than that. Sharon and her parents joined the church. Her dad was a financial advisor at the time, and he tried to sell real estate limited partnerships to our members. Unfortunately, the partnerships were not properly registered with the SEC. We had a handful of members who lost the money they invested in those partnerships. Mr. Gray was convicted and placed on probation for a couple of years, and he paid a small fine. During all this, the Grays moved from San Lucas to Livermore."

"Did Marshall know about Sharon's history with Hacienda?"

"I don't know. I decided I wouldn't tell him because they might have eliminated her because of it. I didn't think that would be fair to her."

"Good for you, Mrs. Kirby. We'll see what happens, won't we?"

"Yes, we will. See you at two."

Matt left Hacienda for lunch, returned to his office at one, and at shortly before two descended the stairs for his meeting with the new church receptionist.

Mrs. Kirby, Lisa Jacobson, Pastor Boyle, and Carlo Barone had formed a circle around the new receptionist, who was standing in front of the table with the plate of cookies. Matt joined the group just as Sharon mentioned that she had majored in psychology. She stood around five feet five inches, had strawberry-blond hair, a few freckles under her eyes, and a prominent chin. Her apparel included white slacks and a pink top.

Matt joined the group and introduced himself to the new receptionist. "I understand you attended San Lucas High School," he added, following his impulse to interview people. He liked to fill in the blanks, as in his crossword puzzles.

"I did," Sharon replied, "and when my dad retired, he and my mom moved to a new development in Livermore. When I started Cal State East Bay, some friends and I found an apartment in Fremont, so I didn't move very far away from San Lucas."

"Ah, I know it well," Matt said. "I went hot-air ballooning in Livermore one day, and the pilot landed in a cow pasture. The farmer who owned the property wasn't very happy about it."

They laughed. Trying to find humor in any situation was one of Matt's favorite pastimes.

"The farmers aren't happy about the new real estate developments either," Sharon said.

"How did you happen to choose psychology as your major?" Matt asked.

"I started reading crime books when I was in high school," Sharon said, "and I became intrigued by how the criminal mind works."

"Interesting. Well, I think you'll enjoy working at Hacienda," Matt said. "Mrs. Kirby is the best, and you'll learn a ton from working with her. Maybe not how to solve crimes, but how to be a great team member of this staff."

"I've liked all the people I've met so far," Sharon said. "I think I'll enjoy working here."

After several more minutes of small talk and consuming three Oreo cookies, Matt excused himself and returned to his office. He hoped Sharon would turn out to be everything Mrs. Kirby wanted. He admired her for giving Sharon a start at Hacienda.

A half-hour later, Matt heard a knock on his door. "Come on in," Matt said. It was the new employee.

"Hi, Matt. I heard you're new to the Hacienda staff as well, so we have something in common."

"You're right. I was here on an internship last year, when I was a senior at Calvin Seminary. I just started full-time about three months ago. Come on in and have a seat. How can I help?"

Sharon took a seat in front of Matt's desk. "When we lived in San Lucas, my parents would attend Hacienda now and then, and I participated in the high school group. I'd like to help with the high school program now that I've graduated from college. Do you need some help?"

"I'm not sure. I'm just getting acquainted with the program. Last year, I supervised the middle school program. Tell me about your experience with the high school group."

"It was run by a couple of adult volunteers. I think Pastor Boyle was relatively new at the time. It wasn't very well organized, but the leaders tried hard to make it enjoyable for us. We visited a Jewish temple, and a rabbi spoke to us after we'd had several lessons about the Old Testament. We also studied some of Jesus's parables. And we went on a couple of bike rides, which were a lot of fun. I'd really enjoy working with the group."

"I appreciate your interest. Right now, that program has a young couple, Mark and Rita Larson, who've taken over the leadership this year. The previous volunteer leader did a great job for about four years, but he was recently transferred to Southern California. Mark and Rita are members who stepped forward and offered to help. They've both been Sunday school teachers here. They seem to have everything under control. I'm their supervisor, but I'm letting them run with the program for a while and watching how it goes. I don't think they need any help right now, but we can see how things go and talk again in a few months, after you've settled into your position."

"My evenings are free these days since I've graduated. Now that I don't have homework, I'm looking for some new activities."

"Great. I'll keep it in mind."

"Okay. You haven't heard the last from me," Sharon said with a smile. "I'm persistent." She rose from her chair and left the office.

*She could be helpful to Mark and Rita in the future, but let's see how she performs for Mrs. Kirby.*

# 15

ONE OF THE MOST INTERESTING LETTERS Pastor Staley received inquiring about the scroll came from the Israel Antiquities Authority. Based in Jerusalem, the authority is responsible for the preservation and oversight of Israel's archaeological heritage. It is involved in investigating, excavating, and preserving antiquities sites, as well as developing and preserving ancient buildings in Israel's historic cities. Richard Cohen, who signed the letter, requested a meeting with Staley in early September.

Matt and Pastor Staley looked forward to their meeting with Cohen. They scheduled a ten o'clock appointment on the second Friday.

A few minutes before ten, Mrs. Kirby ushered Mr. Cohen into Staley's office. Staley and Matt rose to greet him. Staley offered him the chair in front of his desk, next to Matt.

Mr. Cohen was short, bald, and wore a black suit with white shirt and dark tie. Matt paid attention to what people were wearing because he believed it was an expression of their personalities.

"Welcome, Mr. Cohen," Staley said, rising and reaching across his desk to shake his hand. "It's a pleasure to meet you. I'd like you to meet my colleague and a trustee of my family trust, Reverend Matt Beringer."

"Thank you, Reverend Staley," Cohen replied, turning to shake Matt's hand. "You have a beautiful setting here in San Lucas."

"We're blessed to have a wonderful campus, thanks to a generous member who donated the land seventy-four years ago," Staley responded, as the three men settled into their chairs. "How can we help you today? You said you're interested in discussing the Esther Scroll."

"Yes. I had planned a trip to Los Angeles and added a visit to the Bay Area, as I'm interested in gathering some information about your marvelous inheritance."

"We're happy to assist," Staley said.

"When we heard about your inheritance, Reverend Staley, our department was keenly interested in the news from an archaeological standpoint because an Esther Scroll has never been found in the Qumran caves. We were also very curious about how this Dead Sea Scroll—the first of its kind ever discovered—happened to be owned by a middle-class couple in New Jersey. We'd also like to know how the scroll, which was probably found in a Qumran cave, was transported to the United States."

"I've asked myself the same questions," Staley said. "I had no clue that my parents owned the scroll or ever had an interest in the Dead Sea Scrolls."

"Tell me a little about your parents," Cohen said. "Were they religious people? Did they attend a church?"

"They were members of Second Presbyterian Church," Staley said, "which is located not far from where they lived in Paramus. My dad was a high school principal, and my mom was a homemaker. I'm their only child. I'd say we were an average family.

We spent vacations on the Jersey shore and on the New England coast. My parents enjoyed the ocean. I was in Boy Scouts and played Little League baseball. Nothing out of the ordinary, I would say."

"Were they familiar with the Bible?" Cohen said.

"My parents were familiar with the books of the Bible," Staley said, "but I'd say their knowledge was limited. Most Christians in the US don't know as much about the Bible as I think they should. I do know they enjoyed taking Bible classes at church through the years."

"Did they ever speak about Israel?" Cohen asked.

"Not that I can recall," Pastor Staley said. "Let me ask you, what causes you to take such an interest in my parents?"

"I'm trying to figure out why they would have owned a Dead Sea Scroll," Cohen said. "It's interesting that your parents lived in Paramus, which is the home of the archdiocese of the Syriac Orthodox Church for the eastern United States. It was Archbishop Mar Samuel who brought the first Dead Sea Scrolls to the US. Samuel was the archbishop of St. Mark's Syriac Orthodox Monastery in Jerusalem, and when tensions escalated between Jews and Arabs in the late 1940s, he was relocated to the United States to raise money for the refugees in the Holy Land and to help build the Syriac Orthodox Church in North America. He sold four scrolls to a Jewish professor in 1954 through an ad in the *Wall Street Journal*. We wonder if your parents could have acquired the scroll from Archbishop Samuel."

"I've never heard of him," Staley said.

"Given our knowledge of Archbishop Samuel," Cohen said, "the fact that your parents lived nearby caught our attention. The day we read about your inheritance, we went to your parents' home and searched through the dumpster in the driveway. We think we found the narrow box that held the Esther Scroll."

"You went to my parents' home?" Staley asked. "I wish you had called me for permission to conduct that search. That seems nearly illegal." Staley shot a quick look to Matt.

"We called the realtor listed on the For Sale sign in the front yard, but all we got was an answering machine. We were worried the dumpster could be removed. The house was empty when we arrived. We felt we had to act quickly."

"I see. The dumpster was placed in my parents' driveway for a couple of months after my mother's death. I had scheduled some work on the house to get it ready for sale. Did you find anything in the box? All I remember finding was the scroll."

"We found pages of a newspaper," Cohen said, "that we believe were used to cushion and protect the scroll. They were from a community newspaper in Summit, New Jersey. That appears rather curious to us. We wonder what the connection might have been between your parents and Summit."

"I don't believe my parents knew anyone in Summit," Staley said.

"Could they have purchased the scroll from someone living there who may have been a collector?"

"I don't have a clue about that, but I doubt it," Staley said. "My parents weren't collectors. They didn't have the disposable income necessary for that kind of hobby. Besides, we never discussed the Dead Sea Scrolls or anything that scholarly."

Matt remembered that a popular Presbyterian minister from the Seattle area had accepted a call to become minister of a church in Summit, and he heard the employment package included a membership in a golf club. He had seen Summit's name on a list of the one hundred richest towns in the United States, along with San Lucas and Piedmont in the East Bay. Atherton, located across the bay in Silicon Valley, was ranked number one.

"As I understand it," Cohen said, "the first time you learned about the scroll was when you opened the box in your parents' basement."

"Absolutely," Staley said. "I was flabbergasted to find it. They had never traveled outside of the United States, and the Middle East would have been very foreign to them. I have no idea why they would have owned a Dead Sea Scroll. It remains a mystery to me."

"Did they know anyone at the Syriac Orthodox Church on West Midland Avenue?" Cohen asked. "We don't know if Archbishop Samuel sold other Dead Sea Scrolls, besides the four he sold through the *Wall Street Journal*. However, we believe he brought additional scroll fragments to the US."

"I don't think my parents knew anyone at the Syriac church. I'm beginning to object to your questioning, Mr. Cohen."

"I apologize. It's just that we want to learn more about the Esther Scroll, and you seem like the obvious place to start. Our Antiquities Law of 1978 prevents the export of ancient, inscribed objects, so today the scroll would not be allowed to leave Israel. We have strict protocols in place to regulate the trading of antiquities because we want to eliminate the problem of illegal activities with artifacts. We'd like to know when the scroll came to the US and how your parents acquired it. However, I'm beginning to think that finding the answers to these questions may be difficult."

"I have no way of knowing when my parents acquired it," Staley said.

"Maybe your parents didn't own the scroll," Cohen said. "Maybe they were holding it for a friend." Cohen rose from his chair and walked to the window.

With his back to them, Staley and Matt looked at each other with knotted brows, as to if to say, "What is going on here?"

"I haven't thought about that possibility," Staley said. "It's baffling to me because they never mentioned it. If they were holding it for a friend, one never came to retrieve it."

"All I can say," Cohen said, "is that it seems unusual for a couple like your parents to own it."

"I can't disagree with you," Staley said. "The whole thing is a puzzle."

"I'd be interested in hearing from you," Cohen said, "if you discover anything that points to why your parents had the scroll."

"I confess that I expected our conversation today to be about your interest in acquiring the scroll," Staley said. "I never expected you'd be asking me questions about my parents."

"Please don't misunderstand me. We have a great interest in the Esther Scroll," Cohen said. "The book of Esther describes an important chapter in Jewish history, and we'd like to own it. If you ever decide to sell it, please contact us."

"We're happy to hear that," Staley replied.

"I leave for Israel tomorrow," Cohen said. "Would there be an opportunity for me to see the scroll today?"

"Matt and I have a meeting at two, but we can visit the bank this morning and show you the scroll. Does that work for you?"

"The rest of my day is open."

A few minutes later, the three men drove to the bank in Oakland where Cohen examined the scroll. Impressed with what he had seen, Cohen thanked Staley, and the three men returned to Hacienda where Cohen's car was parked in the church lot. It was shortly after one o'clock when they exchanged farewells, and Staley and Matt returned to their offices.

Matt was surprised that the initial focus of Cohen's visit was on Staley's parents, rather than on acquiring the Esther Scroll. However, when Cohen asked to see the scroll, it confirmed his interest in it was more than superficial. It appeared Cohen wanted to keep the door open for future conversations.

———•———

THAT AFTERNOON AT TWO, Pastor Staley and Matt met in his office to discuss Staley's investment program.

"I opened a brokerage account at the office of a Wall Street firm in Oakland," Staley said. "I was referred to a financial advisor by the branch manager, and I told the advisor that I was developing my own investment plan and would be calling him with stock investments to make on my behalf."

"I think it was a good idea," Matt said, "for you to tell the financial advisor that you plan to manage your own account."

"I'm eager to hear your ideas about ten companies whose stocks I should consider."

"To start the process," Matt said, "I'm going to give you a list of twenty companies today that I believe would be good long-term stock investments for you. The companies are spread across multiple industries. Having a final portfolio of twenty-five to thirty-five stocks would provide you with good diversification across a variety of sectors, so you don't have, as they say, all your eggs in one basket. I'm also giving you some reasonable entry prices for the stocks, and most are below their current prices. We don't want to overpay for a stock, even for stocks of great companies. These are all companies that pay a dividend and have raised their dividends on an annual basis. Look at the list over the next few days. Give the companies some thought, and then let's meet again in a week and agree on a handful of stocks you'd like to own if their prices are close to the entry prices I've listed. We'll also discuss how I developed the entry prices I've given you. During your review of this list, don't hesitate to call me with questions. After our next conversation, you may want to start investing by selecting five of these twenty stocks to buy.

"I'll give these recommendations some thought, and I look forward to our next conversation," Staley said. He rose from the sofa, walked to the door, and closed it quietly as he left the office.

That evening, Matt and Jancy had dinner in San Francisco with Oakland Police Detective Ben and Alexis Miller, along with Sidney, Ben's younger brother, and his fiancée, Taylor Holden. They met at seven o'clock at a small Italian restaurant on Hyde Street, near Nob Hill. Sidney had played the guard position, and Matt had played forward on Princeton's varsity basketball team. They had planned to attend business school together until Matt changed his mind and decided to attend Calvin Seminary. Sidney had attended Stanford Business School in nearby Palo Alto, so they committed to staying in touch. However, it had been easier said than done, and Matt hadn't seen Sidney in over a year.

Over dinner, Matt and Jancy learned that Taylor worked in the marketing department of a San Francisco technology company, and her job involved some travel in Northern California. Sidney worked for another technology company in Sunnyvale and said he couldn't share what he was doing, other than to say it involved artificial intelligence.

After a lengthy, but very enjoyable evening, the couples departed. The air was soft, and Matt and Jancy felt contented as they walked away. Approaching their car, they saw that the two rear tires were flat. It looked as though someone had let the air out of their tires. Some mischief-makers in San Francisco? Or something else—and more sinister? Matt called AAA to get some help. They waited nearly an hour for the truck to arrive, but filling the tires took only minutes.

Approaching one-thirty in the morning, Matt and Jancy reached their apartment in San Leandro. It had been a long day, and they were more than ready to go to bed. Their tire problem wasn't the kind of dessert they had expected at the end of a pleasant evening.

# 16

WHEN MATT ATTENDED CALVIN SEMINARY, he became interested in working crossword puzzles. His dad had worked
crosswords for years. Maybe Matt was trying to connect with his
dad, whom he missed greatly. Every day, Matt attempted to complete the *New York Times* crossword. In some ways, he was replac-
ing his daily four o'clock varsity basketball practices at Princeton
by setting aside time to master crossword puzzles. He had found
one cerebral entertainment to replace another, for Matt enjoyed
the mental aspect of basketball as much as any of its other facets.
What happens between a player's ears in preparing for and playing a game can make a meaningful contribution to success on the
basketball court.

Matt suggested he and Jancy might like to work on crossword
puzzles in the evening. In organizing this new activity with Jancy,
Matt decided they should focus on the daily crossword in the *East
Bay Times* because it would be less demanding and easier to finish.
He was enthusiastic about an interest they could share. Jancy had

never been drawn to crossword puzzles, but she said she was happy to give them a try and soon was as enthusiastic about them as Matt. Well, nearly. Matt saw a crossword puzzle as another challenge to conquer, while Jancy thought it was a great way to relax before turning off their reading lamps and going to sleep. After fifteen or twenty minutes of working on the puzzle, Jancy would sometimes become drowsy, and they would put it aside. Matt wasn't always ready to stop working on it, but he wanted to respect her need for sleep. They had been working crossword puzzles like this for several weeks.

When they started their new hobby, Matt had explained some basics he had acquired from working crosswords, such as how they become more difficult as the week progresses. Also, crossword constructors favor words with vowels, so, if there was ever a choice of answers between two words, he usually selected the one with more vowels. In addition, it was helpful to think outside the box. He shared an example with Jancy. The clue was "Comet controller." For Matt, several answers came to mind. One solution might be the name of a household cleanser, while a second might be a celestial body of dust and gases that emits a tail after being heated by the sun. However, the answer to this clue was not the associations that first came to his mind. The answer was "Santa," that jolly old elf who manages a group of reindeer, including one named Comet. Matt told Jancy he believed working crosswords the past four years had kept his mind sharp. He also had a hunch that learning to think out of the box might be useful in his work with the Esther Scroll, dealing with the people who have an interest in it.

Matt kept a small notebook on his nightstand that listed some of his favorite crossword puzzle clues. The Bible and basketball were his top subjects. He had put checks by three of his most-liked clues with biblical answers: Clue: Some of the Dead Sea Scrolls. Answer: PAPYRI; Clue: Fans of the Bible. Answer: PALM FRONDS; and Clue: Perfect Plot. Answer: EDEN.

He also had placed checks next to three of his favored clues and answers referring to basketball: Clue: Avoid traveling. Answer: DRIBBLE; Clue: Jump ball? Answer: DANCEPARTY; and Clue: Fast break? Answer: FORTYWINKS.

That night, they sat close to each other in bed.

Matt said, "I meant to ask you yesterday about your Friday."

"It was okay," Jancy replied. "There was an interesting exchange between a church member and our associate minister when I was in the office checking on my mail. The member was at the counter and mentioned to the church secretary that she had just given five quilts to a social service agency in Oakland that provided services to the homeless, and she was disappointed she hadn't received a thank-you note. The associate minister standing nearby said to her something like, 'Knowing you, Norma, you gave those quilts out of unconditional love, so you really don't need a thank-you, do you?' The conversation between the three of them ended abruptly. I thought that Ted was being rather judgmental and condescending. I'm sure he thought he had helped her, but I doubt she felt comforted by his comment. While I agree with him in theory, I really believe that thank-you notes are one of the most undervalued expressions of gratitude in our society."

"I agree."

"People like to be appreciated for their good deeds. If Norma had received a thank-you note, I think it would have generated so much good will that she would want to become a regular supporter of that Oakland agency. Right now, guessing from her lack of response to Ted's comment, I'm not sure how committed she is to helping that organization in the future."

"I'm sure you're right."

"How did your meeting go with the visitor from Israel?" Jancy asked.

"It didn't go the way I expected," Matt said. "Both Pastor Staley and I had thought Mr. Cohen was interested in discussing the Esther

Scroll as a possible acquisition by the Department of Antiquities. While he said they would be interested in purchasing it when the Staleys decide to sell it, his primary focus today was trying to figure out how Staley's parents acquired it."

"Why was that important to him?"

"I'm not sure. Maybe he thinks it was smuggled out of Israel illegally. Maybe he thinks it belongs to Israel. In any case, we were surprised that he'd pay us a visit to ask questions about Staley's parents."

"It does seem rather curious that his parents would own the Esther Scroll."

"I think Israel is just as curious. They left no stone unturned. They sent some investigators to his parents' home in Paramus to search through a dumpster to find the box that contained the scroll."

"What did they expect to find in an empty box?"

"I don't know, but they think they found the box, and it had pages from a community newspaper in Summit, New Jersey. Cohen wondered if Staley's parents may have acquired the scroll from a collector in Summit or were keeping it for someone."

"Cohen's approach makes sense if Israel is interested in learning about the history of the Esther Scroll."

"I agree. Cohen mentioned that Staley's parents lived in the same town as Mar Samuel, an archbishop of the Syriac Orthodox Church. He came to this country in the late 1940s from Jerusalem and lived in Paramus, which is the archdiocese of the Syriac Orthodox Church. Maybe Israel believes he brought other Dead Sea Scroll fragments with him, besides the four he sold through a *Wall Street Journal* ad, and sold them as well. Maybe Cohen believes that's how Staley's parents acquired the Esther Scroll, but Staley doesn't think his parents had any contact with Archbishop Samuel or the Syriac Orthodox Church."

"Sounds mysterious and very interesting, dear, but now I need to say good night," Jancy said, nudging him with her elbow and giving him a big smile. "Sweet dreams."

After they kissed, Matt set down the crossword on the night-stand and turned out the light. They hadn't even worked on the first clue. It could wait until tomorrow.

# 17

MATT HAD AGREED TO MEET PASTOR STALEY and his wife at the Bank of America branch in Oakland's Kaiser Center at ten in the morning on a Wednesday in mid-September. They wanted to rent a larger safe-deposit box for the Esther Scroll. James and Joan Staley had been customers at the branch for over five years, and it seemed a logical place to store the scroll. Shortly after their arrival at the bank, the Staleys and Matt were greeted by the manager, Richard Kingston, who ushered them into his corner office, enclosed by floor-to-ceiling glass panels.

"Good morning, Joan and Jim," Kingston said. "Sorry for the delay. My previous meeting ran a few minutes longer than I expected. I know you're here to discuss a larger box for the scroll."

"You mentioned you have one available," Pastor Staley said.

"Yes, we do," Kingston replied. "We can make the switch today."

"Actually, we don't have time today, Dick," Staley said, "and we didn't bring our key. All we'd like to do is sign the new rental papers to reserve the box. We're delighted to be able to rent a larger box, but we can return another day to move the scroll."

"That's fine," the branch manager said. "We can transfer the scroll whenever you want."

"Dick, I'd also like you to meet the third trustee of our family trust, Matt Beringer," Staley said. "Matt is a new assistant minister on our staff at Hacienda, and he'll oversee the trust long after we're gone. We'd also like to add Matt as a third signer on the safe-deposit box."

"It's good to meet you, Matt," Kingston said. "We can certainly add him as a signer today, along with you and Joan."

"Now that you've become Bay Area celebrities, Joan," Kingston said, "I'll bet your lives have become busier than ever."

"Yes," Joan replied with a grin. "Jim and I have been invited by various groups to come and speak to them about the scroll. We barely have time to speak with one another, it seems. However, I'm working on some vacation plans."

"I also have another item to discuss with you sometime," Staley said. "I'm wondering what role the bank may have played in reporting my inheritance to the *East Bay News*. That information was never intended for the public."

"That leak was most unfortunate," Kingston said. "I wish I knew how it happened. I can't believe anyone at the bank did that."

"We can go over it another time," Staley said. "Today, I just wanted you to meet Matt and sign the papers."

"Do you live in the East Bay, Matt?" Kingston asked.

"Yes, my wife and I live in San Leandro," Matt replied. "Is it important?"

"I'm only wondering if you bank with us."

"We don't," Matt replied. "Quite honestly, my wife and I don't have a lot to bank right now. We're just starting our careers."

"I understand," Kingston said. "I'd like to compete for your banking business, all the same. Think about it."

"I will. Thanks for your interest, Mr. Kingston," Matt said.

"It's good to see all of you this morning," Kingston said. "Let's sign the new safe-deposit box forms and schedule another day to move the contents."

As Kingston turned in his chair to retrieve the forms on the credenza behind his desk, there was yelling in the bank lobby, just outside of his office. Matt and Staley turned, and Joan gripped the arms of her chair. Three men stood together, each holding handguns. Matt's heart rate quickened. *Were they in the middle of a bank robbery?* The men wore dark jackets and pants that appeared padded with body armor. The bank's employees, except for one teller at the far end of the counter, were being motioned to leave their positions and move to the far corner of the branch. Customers were being directed to the side of the lobby. Matt had never been involved in a bank robbery, and he didn't have a clue about how to respond.

Staley whispered to his wife. "Looks like a bank robbery. I hope one of the tellers has pushed the silent alarm to alert the police." Staley's panicked eyes widened as he looked about the room.

"I'm afraid there's only one door out," Kingston said, moving toward the door.

Matt and the Staleys froze in their chairs. Two of the men charged into the branch manager's office. One had a scar on his cheek, and the other had tattoos on his face and neck.

"We want the scroll, and we want your money!" the man with the tattoos said to Kingston, who backed away from the door and moved to block Joan from the intruder.

"What do you mean?" Kingston asked.

"*El pergamino!*" he screamed. "The scroll!"

"I don't understand," Kingston said.

"We know it's here. We know they own it," the man with the scar said, pointing at the Staleys. "We heard about the scroll on TV, and we want it."

"It's locked up," Kingston said. "It's in the vault."

"Then unlock the vault!" yelled the man with the scar.

"I have one key to their box," Kingston said quietly, "and my customers have their own key, but they don't have it with them. We need both keys to open their box."

"Give us your key," said the man with the tattoos, staring at Pastor Staley.

"We didn't bring it," he said. "We don't carry it with us. We're here on other business."

"Let's go to the vault," said the man with the scar, motioning with his gun toward the open door. "Show me the box. I'll shoot it open."

"If you do that, you could destroy the scroll," Staley said.

The third man knocked on the office window, pointing to the street in front of the branch. "*La Policia!*" he yelled. "*La Policia esta afuera!*" He held two bulging pillowcases filled with bills collected from the teller.

"We know where you live!" The man with the scar looked at Joan, whose hands were shaking. In fact, her whole body was trembling. "We'll get what we came for sooner or later. Let's go."

The three men ran to the back door to exit the bank. Two of them each carried a full pillowcase of money in one hand and pistols in the other. Matt guessed they had studied the bank beforehand and had planned an escape route. He wondered if they had a car parked outside.

Soon after they left, gunfire erupted. Matt heard the gunfire for maybe ten minutes, and then all was quiet.

Mr. Kingston had gone into the lobby and asked everyone to sit down where they were and wait until the police gave them an all-clear signal. After about fifteen minutes, two Oakland police officers entered the branch, summarized the events of the robbery to the employees and customers, and told them everything was under control. The police spent the next hour gathering their names and contact information and interviewed everyone who had been present during the robbery. When the police finished, they told the customers they were free to leave the bank, while the employees returned to work.

Kingston told the police that the three men seemed more interested in taking the Esther Scroll than in stealing money. The Staleys and Matt were interviewed by the police in Kingston's office. Staley reported to them that the robbers said they knew where they lived, and he suspected he had been followed for several days before they showed up at the branch that morning. He had visited the bank twice in the previous week, and it appeared the three men were familiar with the layout of the office, suggesting they knew where he banked. After their interviews, the Staleys and Matt left the bank and walked to their cars.

———— ◦ ————

OVER DINNER, MATT REPORTED his morning's experience to Jancy.

"I heard a customer in the lobby saying the robbery reminded him of the North Hollywood shootout, Matt said. "Have you ever heard of the North Hollywood shootout?"

"Never."

"I did some research on it. On February 28, 1997, two heavily armed guys robbed Bank of America's North Hollywood branch. After they left the bank, there was a shootout. Both robbers were killed, twelve police officers and eight civilians were injured, and there was damage to numerous vehicles and property."

"That's terrible."

"It's believed these guys had successfully robbed at least two other banks and two armored cars. They wore homemade body armor and used weapons that had been illegally modified to enable fully automatic fire. A law-enforcement SWAT team eventually arrived with higher caliber weapons, but they had little effect on the heavy body armor used by the two robbers. This robbery resulted in the need for patrol officers to upgrade their gunpower for future events. Due to the number of injuries, the fact that nearly two thousand rounds of ammunition were fired by the robbers and police, and the length of the shootout, it's considered to be one of the most intense gun battles in US police history."

"I can't imagine two thousand rounds of ammunition being fired!"

"Yeah, and it had a gory ending. One robber shot himself, and the other one bled to death before aid could arrive."

"Well, I'm sure glad you escaped injury today, and I'm happy to hear that no innocent bystanders were hurt."

"You and me," Matt added. "Plus, I'm relieved we didn't attract more attention to the Esther Scroll. I think we can thank the police for that favor. It's amazing how Staley's inheritance has become so well-known across the world. The robbers had done their research. They said they knew where the Staleys lived."

"Oh, Matt, how awful for Joan and Jim. We must visit them and see if there's anything we can do."

Matt hugged his wife. "Thank God for you, Jancy!"

The next morning, Matt read the front-page article in the morning paper describing the attempted robbery at the bank. The three men, suspected members of a Mexican drug cartel, were killed by the police in the shootout. The article stated that no police or members of the public were injured in the confrontation. Matt was relieved the police had withheld from the media the primary motive behind the robbery—to steal the Esther Scroll—and had not mentioned his presence or that of the Staleys.

*Did these three men organize the break-in at the Staleys' house a month ago?*

# 18

IN THE NEXT WEEK, SHARON GRAY visited Matt's office almost every morning to chat. She asked him if he had any work for her, suggested they have lunch together, and even asked for a ride to Carl's Garage to pick up her car that was being repaired. He was surprised by her aggressive manner, considering she was a new employee in an unfamiliar setting. It was mid-morning on Thursday when she once again knocked on his door.

"Come in," Matt said.

Sharon opened the door, smiled, and took a chair in front of his desk. "I finished my morning projects and thought I'd come pay you a visit. Any plans for the weekend?"

"I think my wife wants us to visit her folks in Hayward," Matt said. "How about you?"

"Nothing yet, but I'm working on it. I may visit my parents in Livermore. Ever since the article about Pastor Staley's inheritance appeared in the *East Bay Times*, my dad has become interested in the Dead Sea Scrolls. He's amazed the scrolls were stored in those caves for two thousand years before they were discovered. He's also curious about where Pastor Staley's scroll is being kept these days. Do you know where it is?"

"It's in a safe location," Matt responded.

"What do you think it's worth?" she asked.

"I don't think it's been appraised, but I'd think it would be valued at over a million dollars. It's the only Esther Scroll that's been discovered, so it's a rare item."

"Wow, that makes it valuable, for sure. Will it ever be displayed here at the church or at an exhibit of some kind? My dad said he'd really like to see it."

"He's not alone," Matt said. "I think there are many persons who'd like to see it."

"What does Pastor Staley plan to do with the scroll? Sell it?"

"That's a good question. I don't have any idea what he plans to do with it."

"Who could afford to buy it for more than a million dollars?"

"There are many individuals and organizations that have the money to purchase the scroll. I don't think he'd have any trouble finding a buyer, if that's what he plans to do with it."

"My dad is reading all he can find about the Dead Sea Scrolls.," she said.

"Your dad sounds like an interesting guy. What is his work?" Matt asked.

"He's had different sales jobs," she said. "My dad could sell ice to Eskimos. Right now, he's a manufacturer's rep, selling auto parts. And he enjoys repairing cars. He always has a project going in our garage. Plus, he and my mom enjoy going to Reno to play the slots."

"Reno. Now that a place I've never visited. My wife and I should take a trip there sometime."

"You've never been to Reno? You must not be from California."

"You're right," Matt said. "I grew up in Seattle. I haven't lived in California very long. I've been in the Bay Area for a little over three years."

"Well, I'd better return to the office," Sharon said. "Mrs. Kirby may have something more for me to do."

"I have a question before you go," Matt said. "I noticed you were standing in the church parking lot earlier this week. It looked as if you were writing down license plate numbers on a note pad. What was that all about?"

Sharon's eyes darted toward the office window. "I thought I'd keep a list of staff license plates in my cell phone, so I'll know who's here at the church when I arrive for work. You know, who belongs to what car."

"You sound very organized."

Sharon rose from her chair and exited the room without saying goodbye.

Matt thought Sharon's reason for keeping license plate records sounded bogus. He picked up the phone and called Mrs. Kirby, asking her for a late-morning meeting to discuss the new employee.

About two hours later, Matt was settling into the chair in front of Mrs. Kirby's desk. He looked at her and shook his head with a slight smile. "Apparently, Sharon Gray likes to climb stairs because she's come to visit me in my office almost every day for the past week."

"You sound a little annoyed," Mrs. Kirby responded. "Maybe she finds her work to be a little boring. However, the phones have been busy, and we've had quite a few visitors to the office in the past week. I haven't been monitoring her that closely. If she neglects her work, she may not be here for very long."

"How's she doing?" Matt asked.

"It's too early to tell," Mrs. Kirby replied.

"I have to say," Matt said, "after hearing Pastor Staley's story about La Jolla, I'm a little paranoid about meeting with women in my office."

"Sharon's a friendly young lady. Maybe too friendly. She spends more time on her cell phone making personal phone calls than I think she should."

"I'd like to avoid having unannounced visitors, especially women. I want to follow Pastor Staley's advice and have a witness present when I meet with a member of the opposite sex."

"You could always use my office for any meetings you want to schedule. I know you may feel a little isolated up there on the second floor. I'll tell Sharon that she needs to stay close to her desk, as much as possible, and not wander around the church. I'll also mention that she should call you first if she wants to pay you a visit."

"Sounds good. Thanks for the offer to use your office. I may take you up on it."

"I appreciate your comments about Sharon," Mrs. Kirby said. "I think her visits to your office strike me as unusual and not appropriate. Maybe she thinks you're a handsome guy and has a crush on you. Who knows? I'm being lenient right now. She's in a probationary period, and to be perfectly honest, her job is not that challenging. I hope I can find enough projects to hold her interest. There's a chance she may not enjoy working here and will want to find another job. Right now, we're busy responding to inquiries about the scroll. I know she's doing more typing for Pastor Boyle than she expected."

"She may also become frustrated trying to read Pastor Boyle's handwriting," Matt added, smiling.

"I'll be able to tell in a few weeks if she'll be a good fit here. Let's see how she deals with some of our more demanding members."

"Did you get to know her parents when they attended Hacienda?" Matt asked.

"I really don't remember her parents," Mrs. Kirby replied. "As I told you, her father was convicted for selling fraudulent securities. In my interview with her, Sharon said she has an older brother who lives in Southern California and an older sister in Oregon. I don't remember ever speaking with either of her parents."

"It appears to me that she's trying to create a life now that she's graduated. She mentioned she has an apartment in Fremont that she shares with some roommates. I think she's trying to figure out what to do with her newfound freedom."

"I've overheard her planning to visit some clubs," Mrs. Kirby said, "so she isn't planning to spend all her evenings alone."

"Thanks for offering to tell her to call me if she wants to visit my office. I might have someone in my office or be working on a project."

"Yes, she should have checked with you before just showing up. And how will she answer incoming phone calls if she's not at her desk?"

Matt arose from his chair, thanked Mrs. Kirby for her time, and left her office to check his mailbox before returning to his work upstairs.

At around noon, Matt's stomach started to growl, and he thought about where he'd go for lunch. His phone rang. It was Mrs. Kirby, and he could tell by her voice that something was the matter.

"Matt, Lisa Jacobson was in an accident on her way to the village for lunch. Apparently, her brakes failed, and she ran into a telephone pole. She's at San Lucas Hospital right now, and they think she may have broken her ankle. Her husband is on his way to the hospital. She's shaken up about it, but fortunately her car's air bags worked. Thank God she didn't suffer any life-threatening injuries."

"Should one of us go visit her?" Matt asked.

"Pastor Staley is planning to go to the hospital," Mrs. Kirby said. "I think that's enough for now."

On his way to lunch, Matt decided to visit the San Lucas police station to inquire about the accident.

A Sergeant Stewart came to the window and spoke to him. Matt explained who he was and asked if the officer could share any more information about Lisa Jacobson's accident. He said he couldn't disclose anything about it because the accident was still under investigation. Matt left the police station, wondering if there was any connection between Lisa Jacobson's accident and Sharon Gray's interest in license plate numbers.

# 19

MATT'S PREVIOUS LUNCHEON a few weeks earlier with George Wall, where they discussed the Esther Society, had stimulated his interest in learning more. He called Wall and asked for another meeting. Wall suggested lunch, again in Oakland's Jack London Square, the following day.

After meeting in the restaurant's lobby, they were taken to a table with a panoramic view of San Francisco Bay. Following an exchange of sports news, they reviewed the menu and gave their orders to the waiter.

"I really enjoyed our conversation about the Esther Society," Matt said, "and I'd like to hear more. For example, why is your membership so small?"

"I agree with our leadership that we don't want to be a large organization," Wall said. "We want to have a smaller, engaged number of members who want to make a difference, rather than have a large number of members who don't feel involved. Our annual membership fee is five thousand dollars, so the financial commitment may be a barrier for some who might want to join. Those fees help us administer our headquarters in Jackson Hole, pay for our monthly newsletters, and cover the salaries of our staff, currently seven employees."

"Do you have meetings?" Matt asked.

"We have an annual meeting, usually in the fall and often in Jackson Hole. On occasion, we may hold our meetings elsewhere. We don't publicize our meetings, and, if they're not in Jackson Hole, they're usually in rather remote locations. I think our members enjoy occasionally having a different meeting location.

"Could I join the Esther Society?"

"There's a lengthy application process, including four or five interviews. I have a feeling we're looking for professionals who have at least ten years of working experience in various fields. As I mentioned, many of our members are attorneys. In promoting the Ten Commandments, we want to make sure we're following the laws of a particular country. We also do pro bono work on behalf of organizations that ask for our assistance or can't afford to pay a team of attorneys to represent them."

"Pastors Staley and Boyle at Hacienda Presbyterian hadn't heard of the Esther Society, and each of them has been in ministry for thirty years. Why isn't the Esther Society better known among ministers?"

"First of all, we're not a church-sponsored organization," Wall said, "even though we embrace our Judeo-Christian heritage. We're not looking for publicity. Most of us have families and careers, so it's like a membership in any organization. We're just trying to make a difference without attracting a lot of attention. We're trying to rescue the Ten Commandments from being forgotten in the United State and Europe. We don't have a website and decline media invitations for interviews. In short, we want to keep a low profile."

"Besides attorneys, what kinds of professions are represented in the society?"

"We have members who are engineers, scientists, journalists, authors, doctors, and CEOs of companies. We want to have a broad skillset from which to draw when we identify a project to tackle."

"How do you prioritize your projects?" Matt asked.

"Each year, we evaluate what our overall programs will be for the next twelve months, and we typically pick three themes. Sometimes the themes will continue for several years. This year, we're focusing on kindness to animals, stealing, and the death penalty. The death penalty has been a long-term priority."

"I'm a dog lover. What are you doing in that area?"

"The Fourth Commandment says that animals are to be rested on the Sabbath, and the first five books of the Old Testament, or Torah, mention the treatment of animals numerous times. We're concerned with the humane treatment of animals, including limiting their suffering in the way they are killed. We're not opposed to experimentation on animals to discover cures for human diseases and to save lives, but we want to prevent cruelty to animals across the board."

"How do you do that?"

"We make financial contributions to organizations that support animals, such as the SPCA. We also donate to the Humane Society of the United States, which is concerned with sheltering animals."

"Why did you choose that theme?"

"We see occasional irregularities in the treatment of animals by our meat and poultry producers, and we want to remind everyone to treat animals humanely. To be precise, the Bible's first law from God requires the humane treatment of animals. In Genesis 9:4, it says we must not eat flesh with its blood in it. In other words, we're forbidden from eating part of a living animal because removing that part causes significant pain. In addition, in Deuteronomy, muzzling an animal is prohibited when it's working in the fields, and yoking two animals of different sizes to the same plow is also mentioned.

In Exodus, for example, it requires us to help an animal overloaded with a burden. For these reasons and others, which remind us to be kind to animals, we spend a good amount of time following how animals are being treated."

"A very admirable activity. What's the second theme?"

"Last year, we focused on the Eighth Commandment, "You shall not steal." It's been said that this commandment includes all the other commandments dealing with human beings."

"How's that?"

"While most people think this commandment involved a prohibition against stealing property, it was originally intended to prevent the stealing of human beings. I think the reason the board chose this commandment is because of today's global kidnapping and how people are sold into slavery. It's estimated there are over forty million slaves in the world today, a figure that dwarfs the nearly thirteen million slaves who were taken by ship from Africa. We're especially concerned about sex slavery and are working with global organizations to liberate sex slaves from places like the Middle East and Asia."

"I applaud your efforts to reduce slavery around the world by supporting groups that are trying to free people. How about the death penalty?"

"Capital punishment is a controversial subject these days. The Sixth Commandment says, 'You shall not murder.' Some Christians and Jews believe that only God can take a human life. However, we don't find that stated in the Bible. In fact, in Genesis 9:6, it says that God expects human beings to take the life of a murderer. As the Bible says, we are made in God's image. Therefore, every human life is sacred. Allowing a murderer to live diminishes the value of human life. Having a death penalty for premeditated murder announces to all that murder is the most serious crime. Allowing a murderer to live after taking another person's life is not justice. Just how precious a human life is to God is shown in Genesis 9:6, where premeditated murder is the first act prohibited by God after the Flood. The death penalty is so important that it is the only law that appears in each of the books of the Torah."

Wall retrieved his cell phone from his pocket and typed a few words on the keypad. "I haven't memorized the verses that address the death penalty, but it's discussed in Genesis 9:6, Exodus 21:12, Leviticus 24:17, Numbers 35:16, and Deuteronomy 19:11-13. It's cited in each of the first five books."

"How does your group educate the public about the death penalty?" Matt asked.

"Right now, about half of our states have a death penalty. We place articles in periodicals that explain the biblical basis for a death penalty. We support political candidates who see the wisdom in having a death penalty, as well as elected officials who share that belief."

Matt looked at his watch. He should be returning to his office. "Thanks, George, I've enjoyed hearing more about the programs supported by the Esther Society."

They concluded their luncheon conversation by discussing the Oakland A's and the Walls' family vacation plans to visit San Diego.

"Where do you stay in San Diego? I've never been there, but I've heard great things about it, like the San Diego Zoo."

"We're staying in La Jolla, a nice community north of San Diego, with a long beach for the kids and a variety of restaurants."

"One place I've heard about is the Hotel del Coronado," Matt said. "I'd like to stay there sometime. Have you stayed there?"

"Not yet. Take your checkbook if you ever get there," Wall said, smiling. "You'd really like the zoo. One time we got off a bus tour and saw a cheetah sitting on a table surrounded by some zookeepers. They were telling the crowd about the cheetah and how they are paired with dogs, which serve as calming influences."

"I've heard the zoo is huge," Matt said.

"Yes, and it's worth spending a couple of days in San Diego. The Old Town, a two-hundred-acre neighborhood, is one of the oldest European settlements in California. The historic buildings and displays are very interesting. And don't forget Little Italy. There's an Italian restaurant that is very unassuming from the outside, but when you walk in the front door, you pass by the counter and enter a huge dining area in the back. San Diego is full of wonderful surprises for the visitor."

"Sounds like you'll have a fabulous vacation there," Matt said. "I have one final question. Jancy and I grew up with dogs, and we've talked about buying a dog if one or both of us could take it to work with us. Do you own a dog?" Matt held his breath.

"Yes, we do. We have a yellow Lab named Sunny, Wall said. "We love that guy."

Matt realized there was a good chance the woman in front of the Staleys' house on the morning of the break-in was Mrs. Wall. He remembered she was interested in moving to San Lucas. *Was Mrs. Wall house-hunting or scroll-hunting?*

He'd explore the subject with Wall another time. Thanking him for their luncheon conversation, and after paying the bill, Matt left the restaurant to return to San Lucas.

Pulling into the Hacienda parking lot, Matt headed toward the administration building and his office. On his way, he was interrupted by Daniel Kincaid, the Session elder, who walked out from behind a parked car.

"Beringer, I want a word with you."

Caught off-guard, Matt said, "Okay," and turned to face him.

"Since you're a trustee of the Staley trust that owns the scroll, I think it should be sold and the proceeds used for our youth and mission programs. That would help us accomplish much more than we're currently doing."

"That's an admirable goal," Matt said, "but the scroll belongs to the Staleys, not to Hacienda. I have a feeling that when the scroll is sold, some of the money will find its way back to Hacienda."

"I mean that should happen right now. Sell the scroll while the world is talking about it. Staley doesn't need the money. He doesn't deserve it!"

"I'm not sure that anyone is qualified to judge whether he deserves it. It belonged to his parents, and he inherited it."

"He should sell the scroll and give the money to Hacienda. I want Staley to put an ad in the *Wall Street Journal* immediately. I'm sure the scroll is worth a couple of million dollars. Think of what that amount of money could do for our church!"

"I don't think the Staleys have made any decisions about the scroll," Matt said.

"I want you to demand that Staley sell the scroll, or I'll find a way to get you fired, Beringer." Kincaid pushed his right hand against Matt's left shoulder, causing him to step backward to regain his balance.

"I think you're talking to the wrong person," Matt said. "I don't own the scroll. I'm just a steward of it who's been asked to help the Staleys." Given Kincaid's mental instability, Matt did not want to suggest a meeting between Staley and Kincaid. "Maybe you should write a letter to Pastor Staley, outlining your thoughts. Perhaps you have a point of view that the Staleys should hear." Matt was trying to be as supportive as he could be to someone who was not thinking rationally. Giving Kincaid the benefit of the doubt, Matt wanted to believe Kincaid was attempting to please God through good works.

"I'm not writing a letter," Kincaid said. "I want that scroll sold now!" Kincaid was yelling, and he struck Matt again in the left shoulder.

"Let's table our conversation for now," Matt said. "I'll tell Pastor Staley about your wishes, and I'm sure he'll give your idea some consideration." Matt turned to walk away from Kincaid, toward the administration building.

Kincaid pushed Matt from behind with both hands, causing him to stumble forward. *This guy is out of control,* Matt thought.

Mrs. Kirby appeared on the sidewalk of the church office. "Matt," she called, "your appointment is waiting for you. He's in the church office. Is everything all right?"

"Yes. Thanks, Mrs. Kirby," Matt said. "I'll be right there." He quickened his pace, ascended the parking lot steps, and joined Mrs. Kirby on the sidewalk.

Daniel Kincaid was left standing in the church parking lot.

"You're an angel!" Matt said. "Thanks for coming to my rescue. I don't know how you knew to visit the parking lot, but I'm grateful."

"I wish I could tell you it was my ESP," she said, "but it wasn't. Kincaid came to the office looking for you. When I told him you were at lunch, he stormed out of the office. I had a hunch he might be waiting for you in the parking lot. He worries me."

"You're not the only one," Matt said. "I think he's an accident waiting to happen."

# 20

MATT HAD FALLEN INTO THE HABIT of working late on Thursdays to protect his Saturdays with Jancy. He wanted to be completely prepared for his responsibilities on Sunday when he left the office on Friday and didn't want to think about anything the next day, except enjoying it with his wife. Thursday evenings were usually quiet at Hacienda, and he could focus on planning the Sunday middle school worship service and studying the lesson for his class of fifteen to twenty students that he led during the summer months. In the fall, when school resumed, he would welcome back his two volunteer teachers from the previous year for another nine months, when Matt's three middle school classes could total over fifty students.

He had slipped off his shoes to relax before starting to read the lesson for Sunday—the Parable of the Workers in the Vineyard from the twentieth chapter of Matthew. It was one of Matt's favorite New Testament parables, and he doubted he and the class could cover it entirely in the forty-five-minute period. Halfway through his reading, Matt's mind wandered to the outing he and Jancy were planning for Saturday. He decided he would take a mystery novel in the picnic basket to Paradise Park in Marin County. After their lunch, they would spend some time on one of the grassy terraces enjoying the setting overlooking the bay, and both of them enjoyed reading in their spare time.

When Matt finished the Sunday lesson, he decided to take a break. He walked over to the office window overlooking the parking lot and San Francisco Bay in the distance. Earlier, Matt had noticed the only other car in the church parking lot besides his own was Pastor Staley's silver Lincoln. Matt thought it was unusual for Staley to stay at the church late, given his aversion to evening meetings, but perhaps he was polishing his sermon for the Sunday service. As he was gazing out the window, Matt watched another car pull into the lot, stopping next to the Lincoln. It appeared to be an older American sedan whose paint had faded under the California sun. Wondering who might be arriving at this hour and watching the idling car, Matt saw Pastor Staley leave the building and walk toward the lot. As Staley approached his car, two men jumped from the car and confronted him. They exchanged words, grabbed Staley, and pushed him into the back seat of their car, next to a third man.

*What's going on here?* Matt asked himself. *I can't believe what I'm seeing!* He turned from the window, had to put on his shoes, then scrambled to his office door, and rushed out to Staley.

By the time Matt reached the parking lot, the car with Staley in it was turning down Buena Vista Drive. Matt ran to his car and exited the lot in a hurry, following the older car down the hill. As the car slowed to pass through the San Lucas village, Matt moved closer and was able to get the car's license plate number.

*Is this kidnapping related to the Esther Scroll?* Matt asked himself. He guessed the car was heading to the Nimitz, but he waited to see if it would be heading north or south before he called 911. Once the sedan reached the Nimitz, it headed south. He was relieved that it did not appear to be heading into San Francisco over the Bay Bridge, which would have complicated Matt's efforts to follow. He called 911, reported the kidnap, and provided the license plate number.

Given the condition of the older car, he wondered if it could make it all the way to LA. If they reached San Jose and continued south, he would have to call Jancy and tell her why he would be late in returning home. To his surprise, the car took the exit to the San Mateo–Hayward Bridge. There was hardly any traffic heading west. The car stopped at the toll booth, paid the toll, and continued heading west. There were two cars ahead of Matt at the toll booth, and he kept his eye on the kidnappers' car. After paying the toll, Matt accelerated to catch up with the car because he was now tailing it by a couple hundred yards. The other car stopped suddenly in the right lane. Matt pulled over to the curb as well. Then the car's back door opened, and Staley was yanked from the car and taken by two of the men to the side of the bridge. Staley struggled. Before Matt could exit his car to get their attention, the men had thrown Staley over the railing into the water thirty feet below. Matt's jaw dropped, his heartbeat quickened, and in a panic, he banged his head getting out of his car. The two men returned to the car, and it sped away.

Matt grabbed his phone and called 911 again. He described what had happened and asked how long it would be before they arrived. "You have to hurry; otherwise, he's going to drown!" But Matt already knew he couldn't wait for the police to arrive. Matt got back in his car and drove forward to the spot where the men had thrown Staley over the edge. He parked the car, with its rear lights flashing, grabbed a powerful flashlight located under his seat, locked his wallet and cell phone in the glove compartment, hid his keys under the seat, and ran to the edge of the bridge. The sun was setting in the west, and darkness was descending over the bay. Peering down while using the flashlight, Matt saw Staley thrashing in the water below. The water on the Hayward side of the bridge was shallow, so it might make his rescue attempt less complicated. Matt prayed that Staley knew how to swim. He had not noticed if they had bound Staley's hands. Matt had to hurry. Taking off his shirt and shoes, he placed his flashlight in one of them and stepped to the railing. He sat on top and swung his legs over the edge. For a moment, he stayed there, looking at the water below, and then he jumped into the darkness. Extending his right leg forward and his left leg backward, he held his arms outstretched to ease his landing.

His body listed slightly to the right, and he landed hard on his right shoulder. The force of the impact stunned him. He had never jumped into water from that height. The cold that enveloped him was another shock. He surfaced quickly and, treading water, looked around to find Staley. His right cheek stung from hitting the water after a thirty-foot fall. Then he spotted Staley floating on his back. "Pastor Staley," Matt called. "Pastor Staley?"

"Matt? Matt. Oh, thank you, Lord."

"Are you okay?" Matt swam in the pastor's direction, grateful he himself was a strong swimmer and remembering this wasn't his first water rescue.

"Not sure," Staley responded.

"Don't worry. You're going to be just fine. I'll be there in a second," Matt said, swimming toward him. "Did they tie your hands?"

"No," Staley replied, gasping for breath.

Matt grabbed Staley around the chest and rested him against his body. Looking around, Matt attempted to get his bearings. He could see the Hayward shoreline about fifty yards away. The water's depth, he guessed, was around ten feet because his feet couldn't touch the bottom. However, he knew they would soon reach the bay floor with their feet as they moved toward the shoreline. He swam in that direction, holding onto Staley, reassuring him that he'd be okay.

"The police are on their way," Matt said.

"How'd you find me?" Staley said.

"I saw them take you from the church parking lot," Matt said, "so I followed you."

"Thanks," Staley said. "I'm . . . I'm not thinking clearly."

"I was working late tonight and, for some reason, looked out my window as you were heading toward your car."

"You saved my life," Staley said.

"You're becoming as well-known as the Esther Scroll," Matt said. "Someone has you in his sights. And I'm guessing it's more than one."

"I'm cold," Staley said. "How much farther?"

"We're getting close," Matt said. He continued to side kick and pull with his left arm, heading toward shore. After several minutes, Matt touched bottom. Holding Staley, he pushed through the cold water, trudging toward the Hayward shoreline. Staley was relaxed and floating, which helped Matt make progress. He didn't see anyone to call for help.

"You got a break when they threw you into the water at this end of the bridge," Matt said. "The water here is shallow, and I'm already walking on the bottom. If they had driven over to the west side of the bridge, where the water is much deeper, it would have been a different story."

Matt was wearing down from pushing through the cold water while holding Staley with his right arm. Given their situation, Matt was eager to reach land and contact the police.

From the few trips he'd made across the San Mateo–Hayward Bridge, Matt knew the shoreline on the Hayward side was much less developed than on the San Mateo side. He wasn't expecting to find a landscaped area with grass and picnic tables awaiting them. Matt stood ankle deep in shallow water on a barren, gravel shoreline. Staley had righted himself and held Matt's arm as they slowly trudged up the slope to dry land. Exhausted, both men sank to the ground to rest.

"I was surprised to find you working late tonight," Matt said.

"I don't like to spend evenings away from Joan if I can help it," Staley said, "so it was a little unusual for me to stay in my office through the dinner hour. Believe it or not, I was looking online for a birthday present for Joan. And being kidnapped was my reward!"

Matt smiled. "I thought you were working on your Sunday sermon!"

Staley laughed, as they sat on the ground in wet clothing, facing each other.

Eventually, they rose and walked toward some neon signs beyond the shoreline. Arriving in an industrial section in west Hayward, they found a service station where Matt told an employee they'd been involved in a kidnapping and needed to tell the police where they were. A patrol car arrived several minutes later.

The young officer said, "I need to ask you guys a few questions. I'll try to complete my report as quickly as possible, so you guys can get out of your wet clothing."

"I left my car on the bridge," Matt interjected. "Is it still there?"

"We'll find out," the officer said, flipping open his notebook. "Tell me what happened to you. I have copies of the 911 calls you made, Mr. Beringer. It sounds like you've had an exciting evening."

"Matt and I were working late at the church," Staley said. "When I left to go home, I was kidnapped by three men and driven to the San Mateo–Hayward Bridge. They threw me into the water. My colleague, Reverend Beringer, had followed the kidnappers to the bridge, jumped in after me, and saved my life."

"Tell me what you remember about the kidnappers," the officer asked.

"There were three of them," Staley responded. "They were short in stature and spoke with a foreign accent—maybe Eastern

European. Maybe Russian. When they confronted me at the church, they wanted me to identify myself. Once I did, they forced me into their car and drove me to the bridge. I don't think they said a word during the trip. They apparently had a plan and followed it."

"Mr. Beringer gave us the car's license plate number on his first 911 call, and we're checking it. Hopefully, that will lead us to the kidnappers. Why do you think you were targeted tonight?"

"I inherited a valuable artifact from the Middle East," Staley said, "and it's received a lot of publicity. However, I don't understand how killing me would help someone acquire the Esther Scroll. This inheritance has resulted in a stressful time for my wife and me and for the staff at the church. I hope you can find these guys and put them in jail."

"Here are two of my cards with my phone numbers. If you can think of anything we haven't covered tonight, please give me a call." The officer placed a phone call to ask about Matt's car and learned that it had been towed to a lot in Hayward. "I'll drive you to the lot, and then you guys can head home."

"I hope my shoes and shirt are in my car at the lot," Matt said.

Matt and Staley placed calls to their wives while being driven to Matt's car in a city parking lot, where there were other impounded vehicles. After gaining possession of his car, Matt drove Pastor Staley to his home in San Lucas. It was eleven o'clock before Matt opened his own door. He embraced Jancy, exhausted but happy that he and Staley had survived a dangerous encounter. Matt took a hot shower and tried to put the evening's adventure in context.

*Who would hire three thugs to kidnap and murder Pastor Staley?*

# 21

MATT CALLED HIS FRIEND at the Oakland Police Department, Detective Ben Miller, to update him on his latest adventure.

"Detective Miller," said the deep voice at the other end of the call.

"Ben, this is Matt Beringer. Do you have a couple of minutes?"

"For you, I have all the time you need. What's happening?"

"Last night, I rescued Pastor Staley after he was kidnapped and thrown off the San Mateo–Hayward Bridge."

"You're making that up," Miller responded.

"I wish I were," Matt said.

"Tell me about it."

Matt filled Ben in on the kidnapping and rescue.

"How are you feeling?"

"My right shoulder hurts where I hit the water after I jumped off the bridge, but I'll survive."

"Did the police respond to your 911 call?"

"I didn't see anyone during the rescue, but they found my car on the bridge and had it towed. We called the police again when we reached the shore and found a phone, and an officer interviewed us. Hopefully, someone's looking for the kidnappers' car."

"Okay. Did you see what the men looked like?"

"Not really. It was getting dark, and it happened so fast. I was thinking about a million things. Pastor Staley said they were short and spoke with an accent."

"What kind of accent?"

"Staley said they had Eastern European accents. Maybe Russian. I don't think they were very familiar with the San Mateo–Hayward Bridge, or they would have dropped him on the San Mateo side, where the water is much deeper. I'm guessing they were just following instructions."

"You reported all this to the Hayward Police?"

"Yes. The officer said they would follow up on the car's license plate number I gave them."

"I have a buddy with the Hayward Police Department. I'll check on it and see what they've found. If they have a license plate number, that will be a big help."

"I'm not worried for myself, but I'm concerned about the safety of Pastor Staley and his wife. You may remember the rear-ender I had on the Nimitz. I was driving their car at the time. I thought it might have been a random incident, but now I'm not so sure. Then there was the attempted robbery and theft of the Esther Scroll at the Bank of America branch in Oakland by three Mexican gang members. Now Pastor Staley is kidnapped and thrown off a bridge. It's been a dangerous time for the Staleys. This is way more drama than I expected."

"I hear you, brother, I honestly do. Your involvement with the scroll has drawn you into a dangerous situation because there are people who want it. Because you're a trustee of the Staley Family Trust, you're living in the fast lane these days."

"Do you have any words of wisdom?"

"Like last year, I'd avoid evening meetings. Go home during daylight hours and enjoy your time with Jancy. I'll try to nose around and see what the Hayward Police have found. Finding a car used by the kidnappers would be a helpful beginning to an investigation. Give me a few days, and I'll get back to you."

"Thanks, Ben. I'd appreciate any help you can give me."

"It looks like you and I will have to solve another crime, that's all. I'll talk to you soon."

———•———

ON THE LAST FRIDAY IN SEPTEMBER, after a busy week preparing for fall programs, Matt stayed at his office later than he had intended. He was sitting in his chair, clearing the surface of his desk, when there was a knock on his office door.

"Come in," he said.

The door opened, and a stocky man with a ruddy complexion stood there. He wore a Hawaiian shirt and jeans. His hair was cut short. He wasn't smiling.

"I'm Ronnie Gray," he said, "Sharon Gray's dad. Do you have a few minutes?"

"Sure. Have a seat," Matt said, standing up and pointing to the chair in front of his desk.

"How's my daughter doing in her new job?" he asked, sitting down and crossing his legs.

"I'm not sure I can give you a very good answer," Matt said, sitting down again, "because I'm not her supervisor. However, I'd say she seems to be enjoying her work here. She and I have had a couple of conversations, and she's even asked me if I needed some help with our high school group."

"What did you say?"

"I told her the high school leaders are new and that I want to give them some time to get their feet on the ground before I decide if they need some additional help. I told Sharon we'd revisit the subject in a few months. I'm pleased she asked about getting involved."

"She's a good kid. I asked her to do me a favor and give me your license plate number. That way, when I came to visit you, I'd know you were here because your car was in the parking lot."

"What's on your mind this evening, Mr. Gray?"

"Please, just call me Ronnie," he said. "It's been a few years since I last visited Hacienda. I want to talk to you about the Esther Scroll that Staley inherited."

"You're not alone," Matt said. "We've had people from all over the world contact the church about the scroll."

"My wife and I used to be members here and lived in San Lucas for several years. We feel like we were forced to leave Hacienda, and I still feel bitter about it."

"I'm sorry to hear that. What would you like to discuss about the Esther Scroll?"

"I was born and raised in Nebraska. My parents were dairy farmers. I had three younger sisters. I think my dad hoped he'd have another son or two to help him on the farm, but it didn't work out that way. He was a dreamer and would have enjoyed traveling the world, but my mom was the practical one. She kept telling him that they couldn't afford to travel because they needed to tend to the cows. I think he started collecting stamps from around the world to substitute for traveling to other countries. When he was in his later years, he announced that he was giving me his stamp collection because I was the oldest of his kids. He had collected stamps for years, and his collection was his pride and joy. He told me his collection would pay for my daughter's college education and provide my wife and me with some great vacations. Well, it didn't work out that way. His stamp collection was valued at about two hundred dollars. You could say that my inheritance was a big disappointment to me."

"I wonder why he thought his collection was more valuable."

"He had ten books full of stamps. He put hours into filling them. I believe he thought the value would be determined by quantity rather than quality. He collected the common, everyday stamps available to everyone. I was so disappointed by my inheritance that my wife and I left Nebraska after my parents passed away, and we came to California to find our pot of gold at the end of the rainbow. That's why I'm so fascinated with Pastor Staley's inheritance. Everyone dreams about receiving an inheritance. That son-of-a-gun Staley has become a millionaire overnight! However, you just don't expect a pastor to become a millionaire. Compared to what happened to me, it doesn't seem fair."

"Have you and your wife found gold in California?"

"We've had our ups and downs."

"Pastor Staley's inheritance was a complete surprise to him," Matt said. "He didn't even know his parents had the Esther Scroll. The inheritance has been a big event in his life, to be sure. However, I don't think it's going to change his lifestyle that much, but we'll have to wait and see."

"I'd sure like to see the scroll. Does he ever plan to show it to the community? Why would he want to lock it away in a safe-deposit box? I'd want to have it close by so I could look at it whenever I wanted. I'd probably keep it in my desk drawer."

"It's a fragile document, so there are concerns about its preservation and safety. Also, it's very valuable, so he wouldn't want to tempt someone who might want to steal it."

"I'd be lying to you if I told you I'm a big fan of Pastor Staley."

"I'm not sure I follow you."

"My wife and I attended Hacienda four or five years ago, but several members reported me to the police for some real estate limited partnerships they bought from me. I told the members they were risky, and the partnerships went belly up. I was found guilty of selling fraudulent securities. I was convicted, put on probation for three years, and stripped of my license as a financial advisor. We sold our house to pay our legal bills and moved to Livermore. As my pastor, Staley should have gone to bat for me. I still hold a grudge for his lack of support."

"Pastors aren't in the legal profession, Mr. Gray. I think you were better served by hiring an attorney. Did you ask Pastor Staley to be a witness?"

"No, but you'd think he would have stepped up and offered to support a church member."

"I'm sure he'd hope the members who lost money would forgive you," Matt said, "but I don't know if it would have been right to support someone who broke the law."

"I can see I'm not getting anywhere with you, either."

"I don't know anything about the matter you're describing. I'm just trying to tell you how a pastor might look at it."

"I'm still steamed about what happened," Gray said, "and at the time I thought about burning this place down. As to the scroll, I think Staley should at least display it so the community can see what he inherited. It doesn't seem right that he should keep that treasure to himself."

"You're not the first person who's expressed an interest in seeing it. As I said, he's received questions from persons from all over the world. I'm sure he'll figure out a way to exhibit it so Bay Area residents can see it and learn more about it."

"I'll be on my way, Pastor Matt. I'm glad you had a few minutes for me. I'm sure we'll have another conversation sometime. I've been reading articles about the Dead Sea Scrolls, and I may have more questions for you. I can guarantee you I won't be talking to Pastor Staley about his inheritance. He received much more than he deserved, and to think that he didn't even know his parents had it." With a scowl on his face, Gray rose from the chair, shaking his head, and walked toward the door.

"It was good to meet you, Mr. Gray. Thanks for stopping by," Matt said to the man's back.

On his way to the door, Gray raised his hand, acknowledging Matt's comment.

# 22

News of Pastor Staley's kidnapping appeared in the *East Bay Times* on Saturday morning. On the first page of the second section, the headline read, "East Bay Minister Kidnapped and Almost Drowns." The article described Staley's abduction from Hacienda Presbyterian, Matt's pursuit of the car, and his rescue of Staley from the water. This story became the talk of San Lucas over the weekend, and residents discussed it on Saturday morning while having coffee at the local Starbucks store. The Hacienda sanctuary was packed on Sunday because members were anxious to hear Staley share news of his frightening experience.

———◦———

Matt followed through on the idea that he and Carlo had discussed. To encourage Pastor Boyle to attend the monthly Session meetings, Matt asked him to have dinner with him beforehand. Boyle liked his idea. However, he had a conflict on the fourth

Tuesday of September, so they scheduled a dinner in Jack London Square on Monday evening.

Facing each other at the restaurant table, Boyle winced and said, "Jim's kidnapping last week was terrifying! I don't know if I could handle the pressure of owning the Esther Scroll. There are dangers in owning a valuable artifact! I worry about Jim's safety."

"Someone wants to murder him," Matt replied.

"Whoever tried to kill him must think it would force Joan to sell the scroll sooner than later. If I were Jim, I'd sell it now and move on."

"I'm sure he may be having the same thoughts," Matt said.

"Have the police learned anything about Lisa's accident?" Boyle asked. "Who'd want to cut her brake lines?"

"I don't think they've found anything," Matt said. "They have their hands full working on Lisa's case and Staley's kidnapping. But I'm glad she's making a good recovery from a broken ankle."

"How are things going with you?" Boyle asked. "You saved Jim's life last week, and it must have been a very stressful experience for you."

"I'm doing okay," Matt said. "I still feel like I'm playing catch-up from my trip to Israel. However, I think the middle school program is going well. Also, the Larsons seem to be doing a good job with the high school program. The high school group had a picnic and played softball recently at Panorama Park, and everyone had a good time. And Lisa's doing such a good job with the children's program that it doesn't require much oversight. How's everything in your corner?" Matt asked.

"I can't complain," Boyle replied. "You've taken a big weight off my shoulders by taking over the supervision of our youth programs. Now I can spend more time on adult education and calling on our members. I want to tell you how impressed I am with how you're handling your new job. I confess that I wasn't the best supervisor when you joined us last year, but I knew you were a self-starter and would manage just fine if I left you alone."

"I always knew I could ask you questions if I had any," Matt said.

"That's for sure," Boyle replied. "I hope you know I have an open-door policy."

"I do."

"I'd like to retire in about five years," Boyle said, "and I've been reflecting on my ministry. I've asked myself if I would have done anything differently."

"Any conclusions?"

"I would have worked a lot harder on my marriage," Boyle said. "There isn't anything more important in this world, besides our faith, than a happy marriage. It's been lonely without a partner, and I ask for God's forgiveness every night for not having been a more loving and supportive husband. I was very selfish during my marriage, and that was a mistake."

"Did your wife work outside the home?"

"She did for a few years, but when our daughter came along, we decided she'd stay at home."

"Jancy and I are also committed to our jobs, but we're trying to plan specific activities where we can forget about our work and focus on each other. It's a challenge, but we agree that it's worth it."

"You have the right priorities. I think I would have been a more effective minister if I'd had a happy marriage. Having a partner to share my journey would have been more fulfilling than being alone. I've thought about trying to reconnect with my wife. I haven't spoken to her in several years. Maybe she's remarried. I know she's living in the San Jose area. In any case, I'd like to tell her I'm sorry for being so selfish and ask for her forgiveness."

"I think that would be a positive experience for you. You should consider doing it."

"Now that we're colleagues, I'd like to share my last three Rules for Ministry with you, so we can get this stuff behind us. Would you mind if I gave them to you?"

"I'd like to hear them," Matt said, "but before you give them to me, I need to comment on your rule number five. You cautioned me to avoid working with a financial advisor in the congregation. You also said you lost five thousand dollars in a fraudulent real estate transaction you bought through a member of the congregation. However, you didn't mention that it was Sharon Gray's dad. You could have easily kept her from working at Hacienda if you'd shared that information with the hiring committee."

"I thought it would be unfair to penalize Sharon for something over which she had no control. The Bible says we're not responsible or guilty for the sins of our ancestors. Children are not accountable for what their fathers do, and fathers are not accountable for what their children do."

"It was very considerate of you to withhold your story about Sharon's father."

"On that subject, did you hear that Sharon submitted her resignation today?" Boyle asked.

"No, I haven't," Matt said. "I was in my office most of the day. What happened?"

"She told Mrs. Kirby that she wanted a job with more people contact and less clerical work. She found a position as a receptionist at a Fremont car dealership."

"Well, I wish her all the best," Matt said. "Now it's back to the drawing board for a replacement."

"Yes, it is," Boyle said. "Okay, let's return to my ten rules. Rule number eight is take a meaningful vacation every year. Don't wait until you're my age to travel. Build in some travel to some wonderful destinations along the way. Seeing new sights will recharge your battery. Life can become repetitive and monotonous, so planning a trip every year, even if it's to a neighboring state, can be refreshing and inspiring."

"That's an excellent rule for anyone, not just ministers."

"I agree. My ninth rule is to use your time wisely. There's a New Testament passage in Titus that says to avoid foolish arguments and quarrels because they are unprofitable and useless. In other words, don't spend time with a disruptive person. Learn to discern between a person who is searching for the biblical truth and the person who wants to monopolize your time for his or her own selfish needs. Using our time wisely on matters that are important to God is how we should function as pastors. I suspect that elder Daniel Kincaid needs to criticize others to gain attention for himself. He strikes me as boastful and proud, and he asks unimportant questions, so he deserves less time than others. I like the way you responded to him last month."

"Thank you. I think Kincaid is emotionally unstable and needs some counseling that's beyond my ability. He's trying too hard to please God, and in the process, he's creating chaos around himself. I'm worried about the guy."

"My tenth rule is that we must use our suffering to comfort others. I've suffered from my divorce and from having an estranged daughter, but it has made me more understanding of others who have suffered similar hurts. And it's amazing how often God will use that suffering to educate us. I've thought about how I contributed to my divorce, and I realize how much it hurt my daughter when my wife and I split up. Now I want to reconnect with those persons in my life whom I may have hurt and ask for their forgiveness. Well, there you are. Now you've heard my ten rules for ministers."

"Thanks for sharing them with me. I think I'll be a better pastor for having heard them. I've enjoyed getting to know you over the past year and a half, and I'm grateful for your friendship and support. I'm looking forward to having dinner with you next month!"

"Me, too," Boyle replied.

# 23

Pastor Staley had asked Matt to come a few minutes early to the Session meeting. He told Matt his attorney had learned about a Dead Sea Scrolls exhibit that was coming from Israel to the M. H. de Young Memorial Museum in San Francisco. James Ferguson had suggested to Staley that it would be a perfect opportunity for the Esther Scroll to be shown to the public for the very first time. Staley told Matt that he agreed with Ferguson and would like to approach the de Young management about adding the Esther Scroll to the exhibit. Matt liked the idea.

Staley called the Session meeting to order at seven o'clock. The Amigos Room was stuffy, so someone had opened a window. Staley and the Session clerk, John Stallings, settled in behind a table in front of the elders. Matt observed that all fourteen ruling elders were present, in addition to Pastor Boyle. After Staley convened the meeting with a prayer, he called for the committee chairs to present their reports. He expected the reports to be longer than usual, as the chairs would be describing their goals for the year, following the summer recess.

"Before we begin, Pastor Staley," commented David Marshall, head of the Administration Committee, "I know we're all very troubled by your incident last Thursday, and we're concerned about your safety."

"Thank you for your concern, David," Staley said. "Being a murder target has made Joan and me rethink our ownership of our inheritance. We wonder if it would be in our best interests to sell the scroll to an institution or collector who is better prepared to own such an asset."

"Have you thought about hiring twenty-four-hour security?" Steve Canfield asked.

"I don't think we could afford it, Steve," Pastor Staley said, "but maybe we'll look into buying a guard dog."

"We're concerned not only about your safety," Mike Jensen said, "but about the safety of the staff as well. If someone entered the church premises with a gun, looking for you or the scroll, others could be in danger."

"These are all valid points," Staley said, "and Joan and I will be speaking with law enforcement this week to develop a game plan for how we should function going forward. We've received inquiries from people who'd like to buy the scroll, and we'll be giving serious consideration to these options as we think about the future. Thanks again for your concern. Now let's move ahead with our agenda."

After the seven committee chairs had given their reports, Staley commented that, under new business, he wanted to discuss a letter he received from a church member. The letter was critical of financial gifts received by Pastor Boyle from an unnamed couple who were also church members. "The letter," Staley began, "mentions gifts that Charles has received from a specific church couple that the member feels are inappropriate. We don't want any misunderstandings to circulate among our members that might be harmful to our church. We should have a statement covering this subject in our church directory. I've reviewed this matter with Charles and offered to excuse him from our deliberations this evening, but he's opted to remain and discuss the subject with us."

"What are the specific gifts that the member mentions in the letter?" Marshall asked.

"The letter references Charles's use of the family's second home at Lake Tahoe for his vacations, along with periodic invitations to join the couple for theater performances."

"It would be difficult for me to turn down an invitation to attend the theater," Boyle interjected, which generated a few chuckles.

"How often do they ask Pastor Boyle to join them?" asked elder Karen Hatfield, chair of the Outreach Committee.

"They usually invite me to one performance each year," Boyle said.

"I'm going to limit the time we spend on this matter tonight," Staley said. "I'm still feeling tired from last Thursday and want to conclude the meeting early. Also, I don't think this is a serious problem."

"Neither of these benefits involved the exchange of money," Hatfield continued, "so why does the member think these invitations are inappropriate?"

"The member is saying that it doesn't look right for one of our staff to benefit from these kinds of offers," Staley said.

"These appear to me to be expressions of appreciation for Pastor Boyle's ministry," elder Todd Daniels said. "They don't sound extravagant or extraordinary to me. My wife and I have also been invited to our friends' Tahoe home. We can't afford a place at the lake, so we appreciate being invited. I'm sure Pastor Boyle feels the same way."

"One way to look at this subject," elder Jim Halstead added, "is to consider a minister's service as unrelated to a specific price. Galatians says, 'Anyone who receives instruction in the word must share all good things with his instructor.' I think we should be generous in taking care of our ministers and their families. God will judge the motives behind our generosity toward our pastors, as God will judge the value of our pastors' service to our congregation."

"Those are very kind words," Staley said. "Thank you."

"If I were a minister," Mike Jensen said, "I'd rather receive gifts from the members along the way than have to wait until I left or retired to receive a gold watch. After retirement, how much time is left to enjoy a gold watch, anyway? I'm okay with these benefits that Charles has received."

"I think pastors need to use discretion when accepting gifts from members," elder Bob O'Donnell added. "We must consider the intension behind the gift, as well as whether the giver can afford such a gift. In the case of the vacation home and theater tickets, these activities involved no exchange of money from the couple, only their hospitality."

"Let's take a quick survey," Staley said. "How many of you think the Hacienda pastors should decline all gifts offered to them?"

One hand was raised.

"How many think it's okay for Hacienda pastors to receive modest gifts, especially those where no money has been expended for the particular gift?" Staley asked.

Twelve hands were raised. One elder abstained.

"Well, I see that we have a consensus on the matter," Staley said. "David, as chair of the Administration Committee, will you take our deliberations back to your committee and draft a policy relating to gifts to pastors that we can discuss again at our next meeting? I'd like to adopt a policy for our Hacienda directory by year-end."

"Yes," David responded. "We'll have something to present at the October Session meeting."

As the meeting concluded, Matt was pleased the deliberations had worked in Pastor Boyle's favor. Boyle didn't need another disappointment to add to his ministerial memories.

# 24

THE SESSION MEETING ENDED at eight fifteen, and Matt quickly left the Amigos Room. He pushed through one of the double doors at the building entrance and stepped into the warm night air. The water spray in the nearby mosaic fountain had been silenced at seven o'clock and would remain shut until eight o'clock the following morning. The breeze smelled sweet as he eyed his car in the corner of the adjacent parking lot.

It was the last Tuesday in September, and for Matt the month had been long and stressful. The church was now running on all cylinders. The Sunday schedule had returned to having a nine thirty and eleven o'clock service, after having just one ten o'clock service during the summer months. The Sunday school program was operating at all grade levels, and Matt was in charge. The evening Session meeting had extended his day and left him feeling as if he had just completed a marathon. His schedule that day had involved one meeting after another, and he was finally coming up for air. He didn't care that he had left his desk covered with papers.

Among them was an unfinished sermon he was writing that he would deliver to the congregation in late October.

Matt wanted a reward for his long day, and having a root beer float with Jancy on their apartment balcony would be the perfect answer. As he walked to his car, Matt could see the distant strand of lights across the bay linking San Jose in the south to San Francisco in the north. Settling into the driver's seat, he started his car and pulled out of the Hacienda parking lot onto Buena Vista Drive. He headed down the slope toward the San Lucas village. The four-lane street ran down the south side of a ridge that was part of a range of hills facing the East Bay. To Matt's left was a ravine, outlined by a guardrail, with house lights twinkling a hundred yards away, across the narrow gorge. On the right, a broad sidewalk paralleled the street, bordered by a strip of grass with trees, in front of a rockery and bulkhead supporting the hillside. Tonight, instead of taking the relaxing way home through the residential streets of San Lucas and San Leandro, he would pass through the village and head straight to the Nimitz Freeway. That route would cut his trip to San Leandro by ten minutes.

Shortly after beginning his descent to the village, Matt tapped on his brakes, but he felt no resistance. Then he stepped on them harder, and the pedal went straight to the floor. Panic gripped him. Something was very wrong. The brakes had functioned just fine when he had driven to his office in the morning. Now, however, he needed to find a way to stop his car. He also tried the emergency brake on his console, but that didn't work either. Fortunately, Buena Vista Drive was deserted at that time on Thursday evening, and if he had to drive across the sidewalk on his right and crash into the rockery, he wouldn't be endangering another car or pedestrians. His car was gaining momentum, and he needed to act quickly. It would be a disaster to continue down the hill to the village in a car that was out of control. He didn't want to run into a storefront or a telephone pole or worse, hit a pedestrian.

Heading to his left was not an attractive option to Matt because only a guardrail stood between his car and the bottom of the ravine. If the car penetrated the guardrail, he and his vehicle would tumble into the gully. He decided to head toward the rockery, and he would try to slow his car by scraping along the boulders. He shuddered to think what crashing into the rockery would do to his vehicle. Turning the car to the right, he bounced over the curb, narrowly missed a tree, and steered it at the large stones. His car would be seriously damaged, but he wanted to see Jancy that evening, rather than have her see him at the local morgue.

As his car hit the rockery, Matt heard the loud sound of crashing metal, and he saw sparks fly. The air bag in his steering wheel inflated and slammed into his face and chest. The impact of the nylon bag startled him. His car's forward motion was stopped by the rockery, and the back of the car pivoted to the left, sliding a short distance. He didn't think that aiming for the right fender would stop his car upon impact, but he was wrong. His car came to an abrupt halt and now rested perpendicular to the bulkhead.

Matt sat there for a few minutes, gathering himself and thinking about what to do next. White powder from the airbag was every-where—on the dashboard, passenger seat, and his clothing. He called the San Lucas police station on his mobile and then opened his car door and stepped outside. The path of his tires had left track marks across the grass parking strip. Brushing himself off, he was grateful the airbag had deployed. Without it, he might have received some serious bruises and broken bones, even though he was wearing his seat belt.

Other Session members stopped on their way down Buena Vista Drive to ask Matt if he was all right. After he told them that his brakes had failed and he was not injured, they drove on. Matt said the police were on their way. Curiously, Sharon Gray's car drove past, and she didn't stop to check on Matt's condition. She drove by the accident as if she didn't see it. *What was she doing at the church at this hour?* he wondered.

Within five minutes, a San Lucas police car arrived at the curb, its roof light flashing. Matt was standing beside his car when the officer approached him. Apart from the smashed front end and dented right fender of his car, Matt had not done much damage to city property on his ride across the lawn.

"How did this happen?" the officer asked.

"I pulled out of the Hacienda parking lot and started down the hill, but my brakes didn't work," Matt replied. "My pedal went straight to the floor."

"Have you recently consumed any alcohol?" the officer asked.

"No. I work at the church," Matt said. "We had an evening meeting, and I was heading home."

"Where's home?"

"San Leandro."

"Can I see your driver's license?"

"Sure," Matt pulled his license out of his wallet and showed it to the officer. "My brakes were working this morning. Can I have my car towed to Carl's Garage in the village? That's where I have my car serviced."

"Yes, you can," the officer said. "I'll call a tow truck and have it towed there."

Matt called Jancy and told her about his situation. She said she'd drive over and pick him up. While Matt waited for his wife and the tow truck to arrive, the officer asked him a list of questions about his address, insurance, and vehicle. The officer said he would give the completed form to the staff at San Lucas Town Hall, and they would assess the property damage and would be in touch with Matt's insurance company.

Matt and Jancy eventually had root beer floats on their apartment balcony, but their refreshments were delayed until after eleven o'clock. Matt's evening had become much more complicated than he had intended. At the end of a long workday, all he wanted was to share a root beer float with Jancy. However, as he sat on their balcony, his thoughts were clouded by concerns about his brakes and what he would learn about them the following day at Carl's Garage. He barely tasted his root beer float.

# 25

THE NEXT MORNING, Matt arranged for a car rental, which was delivered to his apartment, and then he drove to Carl's Garage in the San Lucas village. Carl Berge, whom Matt estimated was in his late forties, along with his father and grandfather, had operated the garage at the edge of the village for over seventy years. Carl's Garage was recommended to Matt when he started his seminary internship at Hacienda a year ago, and the two were now on a first-name basis. Berge was married and had two daughters. His nephew worked in the garage office, scheduling appointments and handling payments. Five mechanics, along with Berge, serviced the customers' cars.

"Someone clipped your front brake lines, Matt," Berge said.

"Clipped my brake lines? How could that happen?"

"Real quickly, I'd say. Likely took the guy thirty seconds."

"How'd he do it?"

"He probably used side cutters. Snip, snip. The front brake hoses are easy to cut."

"Can you fix them?"

"Yeah, but you need a body shop to fix your right fender. I don't see anything that a body shop can't repair. I'll give you the business card of a place I use in Oakland. You'll need to have your car towed there. I'll give you a card for a tow company, too."

As he looked at his damaged car, Matt asked himself, *Who would have cut my brake lines?*

"Carl," Matt said, "you're a lifesaver. After the local police, who lay their lives on the line every day, I really admire small business owners like you. You're the energy that keeps our economy going, employing people and providing services that customers need. You've created a good business here in San Lucas."

"Thanks, Matt," Berge said. "I'm grateful to my grandfather who opened the garage in 1949 and to my father who kept it going and expanded it."

"As I've told you, I know nothing about how cars operate," Matt said, "but I'm fascinated by them. If I were to write a book on our culture, I think it would focus on the influence of the automobile on American life. In biblical times, people walked everywhere. And there were long distances to cover. For example, take Antioch, in Syria, where the New Testament book of Matthew was probably written. It was over three hundred miles from Jerusalem. It would take a couple of weeks to make that trip on foot. Now we can travel that distance in a matter of hours."

"The car has had a big impact on our country," Berge said, "and more efficient transportation has made us a wealthier nation. My grandpa's home had a one-car garage, my dad's home has a two-car garage, and some of our customers have three-car garages!"

"How'd your grandfather start this business?"

"Grandpa served in the Pacific in World War II, and he liked what he saw when he passed through the Bay Area on his way to and from Minnesota, where he grew up. He was trained to be a mechanic in the war. When he left the service and married his high school sweetheart, they decided to move to the East Bay in 1947, the same year the Nimitz Freeway was built. Their parents helped them buy some property—a home and a building in San Lucas where they started the garage. Dad was born in 1948. As you know, he still comes to the garage a couple of days each week to supervise things, if you know what I mean."

"My sense is the Bay Area boomed after World War II."

"You're right," Berge said. "During the early 1900s, the East Bay had dairy farms, chicken ranches, wheat fields, and acres of vegetables. It was also full of cherry orchards and rhubarb fields, but they all were eventually replaced by factories, housing developments, and freeways after World War II."

"I've read that California was given to the United States in 1848 after the Mexican American War. Then gold was found the same year, and people came to California from all over the world."

"The history of this area is interesting," Berge replied. "Centuries ago, there were about forty tribal groups, referred to today as the Ohlone. As I understand it, two of the groups lived in the East Bay. Spain decided to settle the area by establishing missions, led by Father Junipero Serra's Sacred Expedition in 1769. The Spanish wanted to protect Northern California from other colonial empires. Over several decades, twenty-one missions and other settlements were established along the California coast."

"The Gold Rush really accelerated the growth of Northern California," Matt said.

"Totally. The Spanish and then Mexican colonial governors, after Mexico's independence, awarded large tracts of land to settlers in the early 1800s. The East Bay had several large ranches with thousands of cattle. However, the Gold Rush changed all that, and squatters who became farmers eventually overwhelmed and gained the upper hand over the ranchers. To support the agricultural industry, factories were built by the late 1800s to produce tractors, combines, hay presses, and other farm equipment, along with a cannery to preserve local produce."

"Your dad grew up in the 1950s and '60s," Matt said, "when all our cars were built in Detroit."

"That's right," Berge said. "As a little kid, he said he could name the makes and models of all the cars he'd see."

"Detroit had the highest per-capita income in the US in the 1960s," Matt replied. "Then, in the 1970s, when we had a gas shortage, car buyers wanted smaller, more fuel-efficient cars, but Detroit didn't respond as quickly as Asian car manufacturers, and it began to lose market share."

"We've had to adjust with the times," Berge said. "At least foreign companies are building cars in America, which is a positive for jobs."

"Well, Carl," Matt said, "I'm glad you're here to help us. I'll let you know what they do to my car."

"Yeah, give me a report."

Matt left Carl's Garage with mixed emotions. He was troubled about his brakes being cut and wondered who could have done it, but he was relieved that his car wasn't totaled and could be repaired. He decided to visit Carlo Barone, the church custodian, to discuss his problems.

He parked his loaner in the church parking lot and walked to the building entrance near the gym, on the opposite side of the quadrangle from the main entrance. Walking down the hallway, past the gym, he came to Carlo's room. The door was slightly ajar, and the light was on. A good sign. Matt knocked on the door.

"Come in, if you dare," said the voice from within. When Matt opened the door, he was greeted with Carlo's friendly smile. He was wearing an A's baseball hat. "Good to see you, Matt. How's work?"

"Busy!" Matt said. "That's for sure. My job description has expanded!"

"Yeah, you're a minister now," Carlo said, "so you have a lot of bosses. More than you had last year when you were an intern. The members think you report directly to them!"

"There's truth in what you say," Matt said. "My official supervisor is still Pastor Boyle, and he's as hands-off as ever. I really like the guy, but supervision is not his forte." Then Matt started to laugh. "His supervisory approach is almost Darwinian—every man for himself. Survival of the fittest. But I think he's changing."

"As I've told you before," Carlo said, "Charlie's a product of his environment. His family was poor, and I think he felt insecure as a youth. There was enough food for the table, but I'm sure he didn't get a lot of Christmas presents, if you catch my drift. He was forced to look out for himself."

"I had an exciting trip down Buena Vista last night," Matt said.

"What do you mean?"

"Someone cut my brake hoses. My brake pedal went to the floor, and nothing happened. I had to drive into the rockery to stop my car. The right fender is a mess. My car is going to an auto-rebuild shop."

"You seem to have one exciting adventure after another," Carlo said. "I thought your life would calm down after Sally Rowland's arrest, but danger keeps following you. Who would want to cut your brake hoses?"

"Maybe someone who might want the Esther Scroll," Matt replied, "but how is killing me going to accomplish that? Really, I don't have a clue. That's why I'm here. Can you think of anyone who might have cut them?"

"Let's see," Carlo said, "last year you were the target of a hit-and-run, then you were driven into the bay in a pickup truck, and then you were thrown into an irrigation canal. Were you born on

Friday the thirteenth? Sally and Larry Rowland were two out of one thousand members. That leaves about 998 more suspects."

"I believe that Lisa Jacobson's brake incident may be connected to mine. Someone could have cut her brake hoses by mistake. Maybe the guy intended to cut my hoses, but he, or she, identified the wrong car. Do you think it could be a church member?"

"Given the worldwide publicity the Esther Scroll has received," Carlo said, "I think the culprit could be just about anyone. Even that Swiss guy you told me about."

"Yeah," Matt said. "He's an interesting character. But why me?" *Could Bertrand Delacroix have hired someone?* Matt wondered.

Carlo shrugged his shoulders. "Your guess is as good as mine, but we've got to keep an eye on you."

Matt needed to return to his office. "See you later, Carlo."

"Yeah, you too, Matt," Carlo said. "I need to go set up some chairs for an evening meeting. You take care of yourself. Stop by my office anytime you want."

"I'll do that," Matt said, feeling better for having visited him.

# 26

MATT CONTINUED TO WORK LATE on Thursdays, allowing him to leave early on Fridays, which he and Jancy claimed as a date night. He liked the solitude of an empty administration building on Thursday evenings when he could focus on his work without interruption.

Tonight, Matt spotted Carlo's office light, so he went to see him shortly after six. Carlo offered a unique perspective on Hacienda's membership and culture, and he had quickly become one of Matt's favorites in the church family.

Surprised to see Matt two days in a row, Carlo said, "You look familiar. What did you say your name is?"

"Very funny," Matt said.

"How's your car?" Carlo said.

"I haven't heard about the full extent of the damage," Matt said. "I plan to call the insurance company tomorrow. If there's any structural damage, I suspect they may total it. Carl didn't spot anything too serious, however."

"You seem to be continually in someone's crosshairs. I hope your life slows down one of these days."

"Yeah, the criminal element in the East Bay loves me," Matt replied

"Surprise, surprise. Boyle asked me to an A's game tomorrow night," Carlo said. "That's never happened before. I just about fell off my chair when he showed up here in my office and extended the invitation."

"I'm happy to hear it," Matt said.

"I think he's taking stock of his life," Carlo said. "He's drawing some conclusions about what's important and what isn't. And I think friendships are rising on his list of priorities."

"I agree."

"You may be having a positive influence on him," Carlo said, "whether you know it or not."

"How so?" Matt asked.

"I think he sees how conscientious you are about your work. As he reflects on his failed marriage and frequent job changes, he may be realizing he could have operated differently when he was starting in ministry."

"You're giving me too much credit," Matt said, "but I have seen a softening in Pastor Boyle in recent months."

"I've been thinking about who would have cut your brake lines," Carlo said.

"And?" Matt asked.

"Nothing yet," Carlo said. "I've worked my way through half of the congregation, but I have a few more members to consider. I must say that you've added some spice to life around here. You've had two attempts on your life this year, in addition to three attempts last year. I think the church needs to hire full-time security for you."

"It'll never happen," Matt said, "but thanks for your sympathy."

"Last year, after the third attempt on your life, you caught the criminal. Maybe the same thing will happen to you this year," Carlo said, grinning. "I wonder if the guy who cut your brake lines also hired those three guys to kidnap Pastor Staley."

"I wish I knew," Matt said.

"You and I ought to grab dinner one of these Thursdays. I'll bet you're getting tired of my beverage choices by now."

"You're wrong about that. I think you're smart to have a refrigerator in your office. I'd like to have one in my office. You know, I'd also enjoy having dinner with you sometime soon. Why not have dinner with Jancy and me next Wednesday at our place? Let me check with Jancy, and then we can confirm it."

"It's a deal. My calendar is open that day."

"I'd better return to my office and finish up. Thanks for the chat. I'll be in touch," Matt said, closing Carlo's door behind him. He wanted to complete his work and leave Hacienda by seven thirty.

Back in his office, Matt opened his window and door to achieve a cross draft and create an interior breeze. It was another warm evening in late September. An hour later, he was close to finishing his preparations for his Sunday school class when he heard some loud noises from the first floor. The sounds appeared to come from the hallway near the church office. He rose from his chair and charged down the stairs.

As he reached the bottom, he heard the building entrance door slam and saw a figure running away from the church. Matt looked down the hall toward Pastor Staley's office, whose door was open. He moved quickly toward it.

As he reached the doorway, he heard moaning.

"Carlo! What happened?"

Carlo Barone was slumped with his back against the wall. "I interrupted a prowler," Carlo said. "He swung at me. He wanted to knock me out. I wrestled with him, and he pushed back, and I fell against the wall with him on top of me. I hit my head and blacked out for a moment. When I came to, he was gone."

"Did you recognize him?" Matt asked.

"He was wearing a mask that covered his eyes," Carlo said. "I've never seen the guy before, but I could identify him if I saw him again."

"How are you feeling now?"

"My head's sore," Carlo said, "and my shoulder hurts from falling into the wall."

"You may have a concussion. I think you need to go to the hospital to check it out. I'm calling 911." Matt's heart was racing as he placed the call and ran to the double doors by the church office and pushed one open, placing a rock in front of it. He returned to Carlo, still sitting on the floor in Staley's office, leaning against the wall.

"How are you doing, buddy?" Matt asked.

"I'm okay, Matt. I'll be okay," Carlo said. "My head's a little sore. I'm sure glad you were working late tonight. I'd be in trouble without your help."

Within minutes, two paramedics entered the building and found their way to Staley's office. They examined Carlo as he sat on the floor.

"It was stupid of me to try to stop the intruder," Carlo said, "but I think I kept him from stealing something from Pastor Staley's office."

The paramedics helped Carlo onto the gurney and wheeled him to the ambulance.

"Can I call anybody for you?" Matt asked, following the gurney down the hall.

"My daughter lives in Southern California. No need to worry her tonight. I'll give her a call tomorrow. Thanks, Matt."

"I'll let Pastor Staley know what happened, and I'll come see you at the hospital."

"No need, Matt. I'll be fine."

"I'll be there tomorrow. Remember, we're looking out for each other."

"Thanks again for your help."

The paramedics placed Carlo in the waiting ambulance, and Matt was left with a queasy feeling in the pit of his stomach.

# 27

Pastor Staley was sitting at his desk, when he heard a knock on his office door. "Come in," he said. When the door opened, James Ferguson stepped into the office. "Hi, Jim," Staley said. "It's good to see you. Say, that's quite a scratch on your forehead."

"I scraped it last night as I was sliding out from under my car. I think I told you I'm restoring a '42 Packard."

"Sorry to hear about it," Staley said. "Well, let's go to the de Young Museum. I always enjoy the drive into San Francisco, along with visiting Golden Gate Park." Staley picked up the portfolio containing the Esther Scroll, leaning against his desk, and followed Ferguson out of the office door. "I'm glad you suggested I keep the scroll here last night so we wouldn't have to visit the bank this morning."

They walked in silence down the hall and exited the administration building. There wasn't a cloud in the bright, blue sky. "This would be a great day for a sail on the bay," Ferguson said.

"We had some excitement here last night, Jim," Pastor Staley said, as they walked across the church parking lot. "A man broke into the church, probably looking for some money for drugs. When our custodian interrupted him in my office, he and the intruder scuffled, and our custodian fell against the wall and hit his head. We haven't had anything like that happen at Hacienda. I'm glad I put the scroll in the safe. It would have been a disaster if it had been stolen."

"I assumed you'd hide the scroll in your office," Ferguson said.

"We have a safe in church office where we keep the Sunday offering before it goes to the bank on Monday. That's where I put it."

"I hadn't thought about there being a safe at the church," Ferguson. "That was a good place to store it."

"The intruder didn't have to break in because the doors were open," Staley said. "My desk drawers, credenza, and closet were searched, but I don't keep anything valuable here. The police couldn't find fingerprints."

"Probably wearing gloves," Ferguson said. "Where's the custodian now?"

"He's at Anderson Hospital in the village," Staley said. "Luckily, he didn't receive a concussion. He's shaken up, with bruises on his face and shoulder, but he's doing fine by all reports. Matt Beringer heard the commotion and discovered Carlo just as the intruder was leaving the building. I'm glad Matt was there to help."

"Drug use is a big problem these days," Ferguson said. "I agree he was probably looking for money or something he could sell in order to buy drugs. What else did the custodian say?"

"I haven't heard," Staley said.

"I'll put the portfolio on the back seat," Ferguson said.

"Sounds good," Staley said.

Ferguson's silver Mercedes pulled out of the Hacienda parking lot and traveled down Buena Vista Boulevard to the village and the Nimitz Freeway. It was one of those picture-postcard days in the Bay Area, with deep-blue skies and plenty of sunshine. A light breeze blew through the open car windows as they drove north on the Nimitz to the San Francisco–Oakland Bay Bridge. Before long, they had passed through the toll booth on the Oakland side and started across the long span, running four and a half miles, to San Francisco.

Once across the bridge, they continued through the city on Interstate 80. After seeing signs for the Golden Gate Bridge and US 101 North, Ferguson stayed right and followed directions to Octavia Street and Fell Street. The freeway ended at Market Street, and they continued four blocks before turning left onto Fell. This was familiar territory to Staley, as he had traveled the route before to attend art exhibits at the de Young. Traveling west, they finally reached Golden Gate Park.

A long narrow rectangle, running east to west, Golden Gate Park has roots that began in the 1870s. It stretches three miles in length, spans a half-mile in width, and ends at the edge of the Pacific Ocean.

Fell Street ends at the park, and Ferguson turned right and followed the park's outline. Then he turned left onto Fulton Street, which borders the entire north side of the park and goes west in a straight line for more than fifty blocks. Shortly after heading west on Fulton Street, he spotted Eighth Avenue and turned left, entering Golden Gate Park. They could see the de Young to their right, adjacent to John F. Kennedy Drive.

Ferguson parked in front of the museum, and he and Staley exited the car. The attorney retrieved the portfolio with the Esther Scroll from the back seat, and he and Staley started to walk toward the museum.

A man approached them and said something, which Staley and Ferguson couldn't hear. The man continued walking toward them, until he was just a few feet away and drew a gun from inside his jacket and pointed it at them. He extended his hand, and Ferguson handed him the portfolio. The man put the gun in his coat pocket, turned, and ran across the parking lot, carrying the portfolio under his arm.

Staley spun around, stunned. He reached for Ferguson's arm.

Ferguson stood frozen like a statue.

After Detective Miller and Matt had watched the robbery unfold from the white, unmarked Oakland Police car in the de Young parking lot, Miller acted quickly and called the San Francisco Police.

Matt had contacted Miller the night before and shared his concerns about Ferguson's advice that Staley keep the scroll at the church overnight for convenience before taking it to the de Young. He also described the break-in and how the prowler was confronted by Carlo. Miller agreed the situation was suspicious. He had offered to pick up Matt and trail Ferguson and Staley the next morning to make sure the scroll was delivered safely to the museum.

Miller asked the San Francisco Police for a car to detain Ferguson's Mercedes and another to help him arrest the man they'd just seen steal the Esther Scroll. Detective Miller told Matt to fasten his seat belt and then floored his car and sped across the parking lot, following the thief running toward Fulton Street. Bouncing the car over the curb and crossing the grass field in pursuit, while turning on the car's siren, Miller caught up to the man with the scroll. Miller slammed on his brakes, got out of the car, and yelled for the man to stop running or he'd shoot.

The fleeing man came to an abrupt halt. He dropped the portfolio and raised his hands.

Miller, pointing his gun at the man, instructed him to throw his gun to the side and lie down with his arms outstretched. Matt ran to retrieve the portfolio. Two San Francisco Police cars arrived at the de Young in a matter of minutes. One car followed Miller's car onto the grass. Miller explained the situation to the officer, who retrieved the thief's gun and locked it in his glove compartment. Then he frisked the man, found no other weapons, took his cell phone, and put him in handcuffs in the back seat of the police car. The other policeman stood with Staley and Ferguson in front of the de Young.

"Wait a minute!" the man said from the back seat. "You've got the wrong guy. Ferguson offered to pay me twenty-five thousand dollars to steal the scroll. It's him you want, not me."

The officer faced the man and covered the Miranda warning before interrogating him. "Can you prove that?" the police officer asked.

"Look at my checking account. He paid me ten thousand dollars upfront."

"We'll do that. What else can you tell us?" Miller asked.

"I'll show you something," the man said. "Give me my cell phone, and I'll call Ferguson's office. The officer uncuffed him and gave him the cell phone. The man tapped the touchpad, a call went through, and James Ferguson's secretary answered. "Need anything else?" the man asked. The officer collected the thief's cell phone and handcuffed him again.

"As far as I'm concerned, we can arrest this guy for robbery," the police officer said to Miller and Matt. "And I think there's enough probable cause to arrest Mr. Ferguson as well. We've got time to figure out this case."

"That's good news," Matt said.

"Let's do it," Miller said, turning to Matt. "You were right. Your hunch paid off."

"I'm sure glad you were available today. You and I are a pretty good team. Something about Ferguson just didn't add up," Matt said. "I'll bet he's the guy our custodian discovered in Staley's office last night."

"Looks like you solved another mystery," Miller said.

"I now have a plot for a second best-selling mystery novel," Matt replied.

"What made you think something would happen today?" Miller asked.

"If Ferguson wanted to steal the scroll, arranging to drive it to San Francisco would give him a great opportunity," Matt said.

"For solving this crime, maybe they'll give you a raise at Hacienda," Miller said, followed by a chuckle.

"I don't think so," Matt said, smiling. "I think I'm still in my probationary period."

Miller and Matt drove over to where Ferguson and the second officer were standing with Staley.

"We saw you catch the guy," Staley said. "What a relief!"

"I'm glad you think so, but he wasn't the brains behind the theft," Miller said.

"What?" exclaimed Staley. "What do you mean?"

"The man who took the Esther Scroll," Miller said, "just told us he was hired to steal it."

"Who hired him?"

Miller and Matt looked at Ferguson.

Staley turned to Ferguson. "Do you know about this, Jim?"

"No way," Ferguson said. "Me?"

Matt said, "Yes. You."

"The other guy's lying," Ferguson said. "Prove it!"

"I thought it was strange," Matt said, "that you would ask Pastor Staley to keep the scroll at the church last night to make your trip here today less complicated. Do you have an alibi as to where you were last night around seven thirty? I'll bet our custodian will identify you as the guy he found in Pastor Staley's office."

"My wife can verify that I was at home with her."

"We'll see what she has to say," Miller said. "Would she want to be charged with aiding and abetting a criminal?"

"As Carlo was being taken to the aid car last night," Matt said, "he told me he wrestled with the intruder and scratched the man's forehead with his ring. Look at the wound on Ferguson's forehead."

"I got it working on an old car in my garage!" Ferguson said.

"We'll ask your wife about your scratch, as well," Miller said.

"I want to speak to my attorney," Ferguson said. "What you're saying is crazy!"

"Based on what we've seen and heard, I believe we all agree there's probable cause to arrest Ferguson for at least twenty-four hours, so the San Francisco and San Lucas police can sort all this out," Miller said.

"Yes," the second officer said. "I think we have enough information to arrest and hold him for twenty-four hours."

After Ferguson was placed in the back seat of the police car, Staley and Matt walked to the de Young to leave the Esther Scroll for the Dead Sea Scrolls exhibit. Then Miller drove Matt and Staley to San Lucas.

Staley spoke to Matt, "You always seem to be at the right place at the right time to save me. I'm very grateful you two came to my rescue. You were the last people I expected to see today. What prompted you to be here at the de Young?"

"I thought it strange that Ferguson asked you to keep the scroll at the church last night," Matt said, "and then there was the break-in, so I contacted Detective Miller for help. We followed you here from San Lucas. I also concluded that Ferguson knew enough about cars to be able to cut my brake lines. He might have cut Lisa Jacobson's brake lines as well, thinking it was my car. Anyway, Ferguson has a big ego, and the opportunity to steal a priceless object and resell it on the black market was just too tempting to pass up."

"If Ferguson was the guy who fought with your custodian last night," Miller added, "we'll want to have Carlo try to identify him in the next twenty-hour hours."

"I think we can arrange that," Staley said. "I'm just shocked. I didn't know Jim Ferguson that well, but I never dreamed he would try something like this."

"I barely knew him," Matt said, "but it's sad that he was willing to risk his reputation, career, and perhaps even his marriage to gain more wealth. We're always being tempted, and this time Ferguson couldn't resist. He may have ruined his life by wanting something he didn't need."

The next day, Carlo identified James Ferguson as the prowler at the church.

# 28

"EXACTLY A YEAR AGO, on October 11," Pastor Staley said, "we had lunch here at Angelo's to celebrate the bravery of our intern, Matt Beringer, whose life was threatened by a church member. Matt became a local hero when he and Detective Miller captured Sally and Larry Rowland and ended Sally's plot to murder three of our interns. Today, we're here to give thanks that another criminal has been apprehended by Detective Miller and Matt. I hope this most recent arrest is the end to what has been a traumatic period for the staff and members of our church. I want to thank Liz and Steve Canfield for once again hosting this luncheon for us." Staley nodded at the Canfields.

Liz, never at a loss for words, rose from her chair. "We're all happy," she said, "Pastor Staley has survived his first two months of owning the famous Esther Scroll. We're sorry that Pastor Staley, Lisa, Carlo, and Matt were all victims who were drawn into the criminal's evil web. However, we're grateful today that everyone is safe and sound. While Steve and I are delighted to host the luncheon for the second year in a row, we hope these criminal captures won't become an annual tradition."

A ripple of laughter swept through the small group.

Staley responded, "We agree with you, Liz, that we'd like to have lunches here under different circumstances. We appreciate your generous hospitality."

"Steve and I want to do whatever we can to support the Hacienda staff," Liz said.

"Much has happened in the past year," Staley continued. "All of you, for better or for worse, have been affected by my inheritance of the Esther Scroll. While I never wanted my inheritance to become public knowledge, someone leaked the information to the media, and as you know, we've been swamped with calls and letters from people who want to know more about it. Unfortunately, Joan and I, as well as others, have had our lives endangered by persons who wanted to steal it. While I never expected to inherit a Dead Sea Scroll, I regret that it has put at risk the lives of our church staff. Lisa, you suffered an unfortunate injury when your car was targeted by mistake. Carlo, you were attacked while just doing your job. And Matt, your life was also threatened by our attorney when he cut your brake lines. And my wife, Joan, was traumatized during the attempted robbery at our bank last month. Matt, because I asked you to become a trustee of our family trust, I can appreciate the stress it has added to Jancy's life during your first year of marriage. Jancy, I never thought that asking Matt to become a trustee would be a dangerous experience."

"I love being married to Matt," Jancy said, "and my work at Montclair Presbyterian has, fortunately, kept me from continually thinking about what's happened to my husband over the past year. I do hope life at Hacienda can become less stressful for all of us in the future."

"I couldn't agree with you more, Jancy," Staley responded. "I hope we can take a long vacation from the dangers we've faced the past year."

"When I arrived at Hacienda last year for my internship," Matt interjected, "I didn't know that chasing murderers and thieves would be part of my job description."

A burst of laughter erupted from the fourteen seated at the two round tables.

Staley continued, "Joining us today is a couple I want to introduce to you. I met George and Anne Wall through Matt, who became acquainted with George because he's an attorney at our law firm. They live in Milpitas, and they're moving to San Lucas and transferring their church membership to Hacienda. George belongs to an international organization called the Esther Society, and because of that, he was especially interested in learning more about the Esther Scroll. We're glad you could join us at our luncheon today."

The Walls smiled and nodded to the group. "Thanks for inviting us to this luncheon," George said. "Anne and I have enjoyed getting acquainted with Pastor Staley and Matt in recent weeks, and we look forward to joining the Hacienda family."

"Detective Miller," Staley said, "we're very happy you could join us for lunch. Thanks for taking time from your busy schedule to be with us."

"I wouldn't miss it. Not only have Matt and I become great friends over the past year, but also, he's made my job much more exciting by drawing me into your crime cases. I've been so impressed with Matt's detective work that I might try to recruit him for the Oakland Police Department," Miller said with a big grin on his face.

Several chuckles arose from the group.

"You can't do that," Mrs. Kirby said. "He's signed an employment contract with Hacienda, so Matt's off limits."

"I don't think you have to worry about Matt leaving the church," Miller said. "He's getting a lot more detective work at Hacienda than he would at the Oakland Police Department. Last year, I thought Matt could have written a best-selling book based on the Rowland case. This year, I think the attempt to steal the Esther Scroll would make a great mystery movie."

"Who were the three guys who took Pastor Staley to the San Mateo–Hayward bridge?" Carlo asked.

"We're looking into that," Detective Miller said. "We have some leads, and we need to tie up some loose ends in the investigation. I agree with Pastor Staley that you've had your share of excitement the past year, and my friend Matt always seems to be in the middle of it. What are the odds that he would be working late one evening, look out his window, and see Pastor Staley being kidnapped? By following the kidnappers, Matt was able to rescue Pastor Staley when he was thrown off the bridge. That good fortune led to our capture of Jim Ferguson when he tried to steal the scroll. I also hope things settle down at your church so I can collect on the lunch Matt owes me, instead of tracking down criminals with him."

"Jim, the past few months have seemed like a story you'd see on the big screen," Pastor Boyle said. "Although I'd heard about the Dead Sea Scrolls, I never dreamed I would know someone who owned one! We're all happy for your good fortune. At the same time, your inheritance has resulted in some unfortunate and dangerous incidents, especially for you and Joan, that were beyond your control."

"As you know, Charles, I had no idea the Esther Scroll was in my future," Staley replied. "It's been a roller coaster ride, of sorts, but I hope we're through the ups and downs and things will even out from now on."

"Did you ever suspect your attorney had an interest in stealing the Esther Scroll?" Carlo asked.

"I didn't know Jim Ferguson that well, apart from working with him on our wills. I did observe that he enjoyed things that money can buy. He had remodeled his home in Piedmont and always drove new, expensive cars. He also had a keen interest in collecting antique cars, which are expensive to acquire and restore. And he had other expensive hobbies, like going to the Masters Golf Tournament every year and attending the Super Bowl. I'm guessing he thought that stealing and selling the scroll would generate some extra funds to support his extravagant lifestyle."

"Can you update us on your plans for the Esther Scroll?" Boyle asked.

"While Joan and I have not made a decision about what to do with the Esther Scroll," Staley said, "I think that holding it for four or five years, until I retire, has the potential for continuing to endanger us and those around us. Several parties have expressed an interest in acquiring the scroll. In the next year, we'll decide what to do."

"Even if you sell the scroll," Boyle said, "will you continue working at Hacienda?"

"Yes, Charles, I enjoy working with all of you, as well as ministering to the congregation, so I have no plans to take early retirement."

"That's great news!" Boyle added.

"It sounds to me," Liz said, "that if the scroll is sold, things will return to normal around here. Then these crime solvers' annual luncheons can cease, and we can get together for more important reasons, such as celebrating someone's birthday!"

"Next year, Hacienda celebrates its seventy-fifth birthday," Staley said. "I think that would be worth celebrating!"

"Let's plan on it," Liz said. "That's a diamond anniversary. I told Steve I'd like to see a large diamond for my last birthday, so he took me to a baseball game."

Laughter followed her comment.

"As the newest staff member, I've been at Hacienda for just one of those years," Matt said. "Jancy and I feel blessed to be part of this church family. I'm looking forward to working with all of you in the years ahead."

Pastor Staley said, "Amen to that!"

# ACKNOWLEDGMENTS

IN 2006, MY WIFE, JUDY, AND I attended an exhibit of the Dead Sea Scrolls, curated by the Israel Antiquities Authority, at Seattle's Pacific Science Center. In addition, we attended a lecture series about the scrolls at Seattle's Town Hall. We were fascinated by their discovery in the 1940s and 1950s in the Qumran caves near the Dead Sea, where they had been stored for almost two thousand years.

During the lectures, we learned that the book of Esther is the only Old Testament book never found among the other scrolls. That fact started my thinking about writing a mystery novel involving the discovery of the Esther Scroll. The story idea percolated in my mind, and after publishing in 2018 my first mystery novel, *What Lies Can Do*, I decided to write a sequel related to the Esther Scroll.

I couldn't have completed this book without a great deal of help, first and foremost from Judy, my wonderful partner who listened to my story, pointed out weaknesses I have tried to correct and improve, and helped me polish the finished product.

Sergeant Ryan Raulerson of the Issaquah Police Department met with me on numerous occasions to discuss police protocol, policy, and procedures. Tom Brewer, a minister who conducts tours of Israel, was my eyes and ears in helping me take my protagonist, Matt Beringer, on a brief visit to that country. Tom helped me describe the sights and sounds of that ancient land. Case Ellerbroek, now living in Israel, also provided insights into the place he calls home. Bruce Mowat supplied helpful information about the San Francisco Bay Area, which is the setting for both of my mystery novels, even though I haven't lived there in almost fifty years. Jim Flaggert, a Seattle attorney, helped me understand Matt's responsibilities as a trustee. Brad Connell, an expert car mechanic, answered questions I had about how an automobile operates. I also owe a great debt to Dennis Prager, whose commentary on Genesis has been an inspiration to me. He's an expert on the Torah and the Ten Commandments, and his wisdom was incorporated into my story.

The person who helped me pull the story together is my editor, Christine Breen, who was the invaluable editor of my first mystery novel. As a published author, her experience and expertise also guided me through the completion of my second novel. I also had helpful support from Melissa Coffman and Scott Book at Book House Publishing. Melissa coordinated the publishing, Scott designed the cover, and their team member, Julie Scandora, provided excellent editing of my manuscript. I have many team members to thank, and I'm grateful for their assistance.

# ABOUT THE AUTHOR

ERICK LEITHE WAS RAISED in Seattle, Washington. After graduating from Princeton University, he attended the San Francisco Theological Seminary in San Anselmo, California, where he earned Master of Divinity and Doctor of Ministry degrees. For thirty-seven years, he was a financial advisor for a major Wall Street investment firm, retiring in 2019. He published his first mystery novel, *What Lies Can Do*, in 2018. His second mystery novel, *Secret Motives*, is a sequel. He and his wife, Judy, live in Issaquah, Washington, near Seattle.

Made in the USA
Monee, IL
21 November 2022

18277098R00142